JUNGLE RUN

Despite the blurriness of his right eye, Frost could make out a path ahead of him. He slowed to a halt and tried to see from side to side. Then he darted across the path and crouched in the brush beyond it. He waited, the wooden spear in his right hand raised in anticipation. . . .

The last of the Communist guerillas was even with Frost now. Frost raised the spear, stepped from behind the trunk of the tree and hammered the spear forward.

"Aagh!"

The guerilla toppled forward. Frost dropped on the man's back, wrenched the spear free, and drove it down again—between the man's shoulder blades. But the vision in Frost's eye was worse for the exertion, and the guerilla party was doubling back. Frost would have to fight blindly, so to speak. He pumped the trigger on the Communist assault rifle as another man rounded the elbow of the trail. Frost's rifle pursued the man, and those who followed, with a long burst that nearly ripped the right arm from the man's shoulder, the arteries in the neck spurting blood. Frost dropped to his knees, snatching at the belt of the man he'd speared, finding one, then another, spare magazine. There was a machete too, and Frost groped for it, trying to discern his next approaching victim. . . .

ADVENTURE THROUGH WORLD WAR II

THE SGT. #1: DEATH TRAIL (600, $2.25)
by Gordon Davis
The first in the dynamic World War II series featuring the action crammed exploits of the Sergeant, C.J. Mahoney. With a handful of *maquis*, Mahoney steals an explosive laden train and heads for a fateful rendezvous in a tunnel of death!

THE SGT. #2: HELL HARBOR (623, $2.25)
by Gordon Davis
Tough son-of-a-gun Mahoney leaves a hospital bed to fulfill his assignment: he must break into an impregnable Nazi fortress to disarm the detonators that could blow Cherbourg Harbor—and himself—to doom. . . .

THE SGT. #3: BLOODY BUSH (647, $2.25)
by Gordon Davis
C.J. Mahoney is sent to save an entire company from being torn apart in Normandy's savage Battle of the Hedgerows. And if the vicious panzers don't get him, the vengeful Yank commander will. . . .

IN SEARCH OF EAGLES (913, $2.50)
by Christopher Sloan
The breathtaking drama of World War II dogfights comes back to life when Captain James Sutton undertakes an incredible mission. The chances for survival are minimal, but Sutton is born for the glory of the air!

Available wherever paperbacks are sold, or order direct from the Publisher. Send cover price plus 50¢ per copy for mailing and handling to Zebra Books, 475 Park Avenue South, New York, N.Y. 10016. DO NOT SEND CASH.

#10

THEY CALL ME
THE
MERCENARY
BUSH WARFARE
BY AXEL KILGORE

ZEBRA BOOKS
KENSINGTON PUBLISHING CORP.

ZEBRA BOOKS

are published by

KENSINGTON PUBLISHING CORP.
475 Park Avenue South
New York, N.Y. 10016

Printed in the United States of America

To Laverne, whose nimble fingers keep Hank Frost going.

Chapter 1

Frost's tongue stuck to the roof of his mouth. "Dry . . ." He started to choke, opening his right eye as he sat up. He squinted his eye shut tight—blurring.

He opened his eye again. The blurriness was going, but there was something odd about it still, the blurriness not a bleary-eyed early morning feeling. He squinted it shut once more, then opened it. His vision was clear.

Frost looked about him—rain forest. High, sucker-shaped trees closed over his head, making a canopy and shielding him from the sun. Only spearlike shafts of the sunlight filtered down, dust particles floating in them near the ground. The tree trunks were largely bare—jungle. The ground under him was soft, springy, damp. There was some kind of bug crawling up his left arm and he swatted it away with his right hand. Dark bruises—two of them—were in the crook of his left elbow. He squinted to look at them closely—needle marks?

Blurriness again. The one-eyed man squinted his right eye shut, shaking his head to clear it. "Injection," he rasped, starting to cough again, his head hurting. The jacket from his white suit was on the ground and he reached across to it, shaking it, checking under the lapels, in the lining, that something unfriendly hadn't taken up residence there.

The jacket felt light—no spare magazines for the Browning or speedloaders for the Metalife Custom. He leaned back on his elbows, remembering. There was no spare ammo because the Metalife Custom .357 was in London locked in Bess's office safe. The Browning was still in the United States, where he'd left it. So was the Gerber boot knife. He shook his head again, "But I wasn't in the damn jun—" He looked up, at the high treetops, then around him, starting to his feet, too quickly, his head aching, the vision in his right eye blurring. He felt something on the front of his shirt.

A piece of paper—tacked to his shirt front like a child's note from school. He pulled the straight pin out and tossed it away, squinting to study the note. Something about the spidery, almost calligraphic handwriting struck him as familiar, something he'd seen, but a long time ago:

The injection we have given you will induce permanent blindness in seventy-two hours. The jungle itself, the beasts and snakes, Communist terrorists and your already blurr-

8

ing vision stand between you and the house my father built . . .

Frost looked at the dark bruises on his left arm, swallowing hard, feeling the blurriness again in his right eye. "Psychosomatic," he murmured, then squinted hard, the blurriness passing. It wasn't psychosomatic. He continued to read the note.

. . . my father built. (Read that part, dammit!) I am surrounded by armed men, attack dogs, electronic defense systems. I have the antidote for the injection. Come to me . . .

He studied the name at the bottom of the note—elaborate, Germanic—she had been raised there, Frost remembered. He said the name aloud. "Eva Chapmann."

A flood of memories washed over him. Colonel Marcus Chapmann, Latin America and the slaughter there—Selman, Colonel Tarleton, Major Grist—the night in that other jungle, the bats coming to suck the blood from the bodies of all the dead there in the village square. Frost closed his eye, remembering the gunships when they'd come, Selman trying to save him. The bullets that had ripped through Frost's legs. A smile crossed the one-eyed man's lips. He remembered the nun who had cared for him at the mission. She'd told him then, ". . . revenge will only harden your heart—that's not God's way." And Frost remembered what he'd answered, remembered the

9

look on her face. ". . . revenge couldn't harden my heart. That massacre by Chapmann's men . . . did that. And if you're right and God kept me alive there's only one purpose I can see for it . . . revenge is all I give right now." And the one-eyed man had gotten the revenge, weeks and thousands of miles later in Switzerland . . .

Frost fired once, then again, the first shot boring into Chapmann's right elbow, the second shot into his right knee. There was a scream of pain . . . Frost smiled, watching Chapmann's reaction and growing terror. Chapmann's china blue eyes were like little pinpoints of fear: there was blood running from the right corner of his mouth—apparently he had hit his face when he had fallen. . . . Chapmann started to crawl toward his gun. Frost let him go for it. As Colonel Marcus Chapmann reached for his pistol and started to turn, pointing it toward Frost, Frost said, "One hundred and fifty of my friends—you killed them, left me for dead, but now you're the one." Frost fired once, then once more into Chapmann's chest and Chapmann fell back, head down along the steps. Frost walked down the steps and dropped to one knee beside him. Methodically, Frost pulled Chapmann's head forward, pushed the muzzle of his silenced pistol to Chapmann's exposed neck, against the spinal column. Then Frost fired his pistol twice . . .*

Frost closed his eye, then opened it. It was Chapmann's daughter now—and once again it was revenge, but Eva Chapmann's revenge against the man who had killed her father. The one-eyed man thought about it for a moment. If he died, out in the African jungle and alone, blind . . . Having killed Marcus Chapmann, exterminated him like a vermin-carrying rodent, would still have made it all worthwhile.

Frost pushed himself to his feet finally. "Eva Chapmann," he muttered.

He swayed on his feet, his head aching. He looked down at his left arm, just below the rolled up shirt sleeve. Two injection marks—one apparently to knock him out. He glanced at the black faced Rolex Sea-Dweller on his left wrist. At least they hadn't taken his watch. He smiled at his own naivete. But of course they'd left the watch. Seventy-one hours or so remained if he'd been given the injection when they first got him into the bush. They wanted him to know the time, count the hours, then the minutes—as long as he could see the face of the watch. He looked at the note again. Beneath the name Eva Chapmann was a finely drawn but crude, barebones map. She wanted him to come—or perhaps just die trying.

"Seventy-one hours—yes," he murmured.

He still had his cigarettes and his Zippo lighter. He put one of the cigarettes in the left corner of

*See, They Call Me The Mercenary #1, The Killer Genesis

11

his mouth, then rolled the striking wheel of the Zippo under his thumb. It sparked, lighting. Frost inhaled the smoke deep into his lungs. Under the circumstances, there was no sense worrying about carcinogens, he decided.

Frost found a fresh deadfall tree branch, thick at the base and tapering toward the end. Using a small slab of rock, he hewed away the rest of the branches and began working the end into a sharp point. He eyed some of the vines not far above him. Three of them could be braided into a rope. A spear and a rope—the one-eyed man smiled.

Definitely—under the circumstances, there was no sense worrying about carcinogens.

Chapter 2

As he started moving across the jungle, Frost looked down at his sixty-five dollar shoes—they were already showing signs of the rough terrain. He clambered over a rotted, termite-infested tree trunk, ducking under low hanging vines, trying to follow the course of the sun. . . .

After the shootout at the seaside country house in England and finding Bess there, still alive,* both of them had felt that getting away was something they needed—time together to sort out their lives. When Frost had been in the suburban London hospital before that, his mail had caught up with him. And one item had caught his imagination, the reunion of an old outfit, the one he'd served with in Rhodesia when he'd first become a mercenary. Spinner, Caruthers, Tushingham, Galt—all of the guys he hadn't seen in years were to be there in South Africa. A good way of in-

*See, They Call Me The Mercenary #9, The Terror Contract

troducing his girl to the men who'd so quickly in those early days become his friends. He'd been surprised at the time, thinking there weren't enough left of the outfit. They'd fought as a unit—Frost had gone his own way by then—twice in Africa and once more in Latin America. He'd thought most of them were dead. The possibility of a reunion, then, had been doubly meaningful and South Africa had seemed the logical choice—the only place left where it would be safe to hold it. . . .

He had gone down to the lobby for a fresh pack of cigarettes, leaving Bess in the room. Though the hotel had been booked, none of his friends had arrived yet. Frost had already rationalized that—he and Bess had gotten there thirty-six hours early. On the way back to the room, he had passed a bellboy wheeling a large trunk on a dolly. The bellboy had partially blocked the corridor and Frost remembered starting around him, then suddenly feeling nausea and smelling something like rotted flowers. And that was all he remembered . . .

Frost broke through into a clearing and stared skyward. The sun was lower now. For the last hour, he had been following the signs of men moving through the jungle, not knowing if they were Eva Chapmann's men or some of the Communist terrorists to whom she'd referred in the note. But he knew the terrain in a general way. He was hundreds of miles north of the savannas now, in a lowland river basin jungle. He wasn't even quite certain what country he was in.

Frost kept walking. His vision began to blur once and he rested beside a tree trunk for a time. "Exertion—exertion does it," he rasped to himself. Squinting, he saw a black mamba—enough venom to kill ten men—less than a yard from him, ready to strike. The spear made from the tree limb was beside his right arm, against the tree trunk by which he sat. Slowly, eyeing the poised mamba, Frost reached his hand back for the spear. "Like some damn caveman," he muttered, smiling at the snake. The black mamba didn't move. Frost's right fist knotted around the shaft of the spear. The snake twitched. Frost boosted the spear into an arc across the front of his body, knifing it down toward the ground, rolling his body away from the tree trunk as the snake sprang. The crude wooden point of the spear struck the snake, glancing off its body, deflecting the snake's strike. On his feet, Frost snatched up a rock, hurling it toward the ground and at the mamba's head.

He edged back, his vision blurring badly, dizziness and nausea sweeping over him. He could barely see the snake. It wasn't moving. Frost reached down and grabbed up his spear. He squinted his right eye tightly shut, then tried to read the blurred face of his wristwatch. Six hours had passed. "Seventy-two hours my ass," he muttered, catching up his braided vine rope. As he started walking again, the dizziness passing but his vision not quite clear, he decided that if something didn't happen to stop it, for all intents and purposes he'd be virtually blind in another six to eight

15

hours—just when the African night would fall.

Another hour had passed, the blurriness of his vision not going fully. But he could see well enough, Frost thought. And subconsciously, as his vision had deteriorated throughout the day, he had found himself listening, feeling, smelling things with greater awareness. When he had lost his left eye years back in Viet Nam, he had for a while become obsessed with the possibility of total blindness—obsessed and terrified. He had taught himself to read rudimentary braille, practiced for a time going about his apartment later with his other eye blindfolded, trying to learn to move by feel. He'd taught himself to shoot with his right eye closed too—at targets short distances away, center of mass shots on full sized silhouettes at seven to ten yards.

But the jungle itself was the enemy. Had he encountered the black mamba and been unable to see to defend himself, it would have been the end—

He thought of the Ringhals snake inhabiting the southern regions. He smiled—the usual effect of the Ringhals' spitted venom was blindness. Poetic justice, he wondered, or irony?

Frost stopped cold, beside a moss-laden tree, listening. It had been a human sound—a cough, then another. Chapmann's daughter's men? Frost crouched, listening. Had Bess alerted the local police hundreds of miles away? Were they looking for him? Had the reunion of his old merc unit been a set-up by Eva Chapmann, just to get him, or had the reunion actually been planned and Eva

Chapmann merely used it? Those were questions Frost couldn't answer. If Bess were all right, that was the important thing. A police search would not extricate him from the jungle. And even if by some miracle he were rescued, it would be doubtful that blood tests could determine the exact nature of the drug he had been administered—and the blindness would come.

"Hank Frost, blind security guard," Frost whispered to himself, under his breath.

He didn't like the ring of it—blind anything. If they were Chapmann's men, perhaps they carried the antidote for the drug—just in case. And if they weren't, the source of the human sounds he heard were likely Communist terrorists. They would be well-armed. Frost needed a gun, a decent knife—food, water that would be drinkable.

He edged forward, away from the tree trunk, parting the foliage in front of him, peering through the niche in the broad green leaves. Six men, all black, AK-47s under their arms—Communist. The man bringing up the rear of the single file was a little shorter than the others—Frost decided that would be good.

Slowly, Frost let the leaves close in front of him, then started moving along parallel lines to the rough jungle track the six men followed. He clambered up a small rise of ground, over green moss-coated rocks and down, through a stand of gnarled trees, then started to run across a small clearing, still paralleling the trail, but far enough away from it that the sounds he might make would be thought animal noises—perhaps a bongo running from cover, or a Congo peafowl.

There was a gorge in the ground—a tiny rivulet in the rainy season, he surmised. He jumped it, broke through a patch of thorn bushes and continued running. He could see the path ahead, despite the blurriness of his right eye. He slowed, stopped, looked from side to side. There was a large-trunked tree across the track. No sign of the Communist guerillas. He streaked across the path and down behind it. He waited.

He could hear the coughing again, then somebody laughing. The six men were coming. The trail elbowed sharply just past where Frost waited. He was counting on that to buy him time. And the trail was steep here, too—that would widen the gap in the file as they walked.

Frost waited, the wooden spear in his right hand.

The lead man walked past, less than a yard from him—Frost held his breath.

The second man, then the third and fourth.

It was the fifth man who was coughing—Frost heard him, saw him. The fifth man moved past, the sixth man, the short one, coming.

The sixth man was even with Frost now—under the camouflage foraging cap, Frost could see the hair—reddish tinged in the patches of sunlight. Frost mentally shrugged. The black eyes were wide, sweat streaming down the man's face, making his skin glisten.

He was two paces past Frost, the fifth man already past the elbow in the trail, out of sight.

Frost raised the spear, stepped from behind the

trunk of the tree and hammered the spear forward.

"Aagh!"

The guerilla toppled forward. Frost fell on his back, wrenching out the spear, driving it down again between the shoulder blades. "Aagh—gh!"

"Eat wood, sucker," Frost rasped, loosing the spear and unraveling the sling of the AK-47 from the dead man's right shoulder.

"Binke! Binke!"

It had to be the fifth man—the voice was so close.

Frost had the AK, worked the bolt and swept the muzzle up.

Frost squinted his right eye, tight shut—the blurring again. He pumped the trigger on the Communist assault rifle as the fifth man rounded the elbow in the trail, a long burst, ragged because of the way Frost held the rifle, almost ripping the fifth man's right arm away at the shoulder, the arteries in the neck spurting blood.

Frost was on his knees, snatching at the belt of the man he'd speared, finding one, then another spare magazine. There was a machete on the belt—he grabbed it.

On his feet, Frost fired another burst from the AK-47—the fourth man in the file was already around the elbow in the trail, firing, the leaves in the foliage near Frost's head shredding. Frost fired a burst, the guerilla wheeling, his eyes wide, terrified as he realized he was hit, doubling over and rolling back into the foliage.

"Food—water—nuts!" Frost started to run,

back along the trail, hearing shouting, gunfire behind him.

There were still three of the Communist guerrillas. Frost jumped a rotted, termite ridden tree, his left foot catching as he went down. He rolled onto his back, the AK swinging into position.

The third man in the terrorist file was streaking toward him. Frost fired, the terrorists firing too. The log exploded, termites and wood chips filling the air, but the third man going down.

Frost brushed the stuff away—"Shit!" On his knees, he fired at the first and second men, the two men diving to opposite sides of the trail, returning fire. Frost hunkered down behind what was left of the log and loosed another burst.

He heard a dull, thudding sound, glanced to his right. He squinted his eye tight shut, then opened it. "Grenade," he rasped, pushing himself to his feet and diving into the foliage. The ground shuddered behind him, dirt streaming down on him like rain.

The two terrs were up, running. Frost—his left arm bleeding, feeling blood on his face, rolled onto his back, sweeping the AK-47 in a broad arc.

"You fuckin' . . ." It was one of the guerillas, shouting as he doubled over and went down.

The last man jumped toward Frost, the man's rifle apparently empty or anger overruling his common sense. Frost made to fire the AK—"Empty!"

Frost rolled and the man hit the dirt.

The guerilla was on his feet, lunging, hands oustretched.

Frost snatched for the machete stuffed in his belt and sliced it through the air, the blade edge catching the center of the man's face, exploding in blood.

The last man went down, Frost falling onto him, using the butt of the machete like a karate stick, hammering it with all his strength into the exposed left temple. There was a groan, the tension in the body under him dissolving. He looked down across the length of the body—the camouflage pants were staining dark and wet.

Frost fell back on his haunches. He closed his eye. "Food—water—ammo," he rasped. When he opened his eye, the blurring was pronouncedly worsened—and he was very tired.

Chapter 3

Taking a hat, even some of the clothes of the dead men would have been wise, the one-eyed man reflected—but two of the men had had head lice and what else they carried in their clothes he didn't want to find out. The food was useless to him—half rotted, but the water seemed clean enough.

With two AK-47s, a Webley revolver in .38-200 (200-grain .38 Smith & Wesson), assorted knives, plenty of ammo and a compass, Frost started out along the trail. He wanted to rest—it was growing dark but he couldn't. The blindness in his right eye seemed to be increasing by the minute—within another few hours, it would be total or nearly so. If he slept, he might awaken totally blind.

Frost kept moving. The trail he followed was the trail outlined on the map; since Eva Chapmann had provided the map, Frost had no illusion the trail was safe. That was, after all, the idea—that he should "die trying," turn his single virtue—stubbornness—against himself to bring about his own destruction. . . .

The black faced Rolex Sea-Dweller—he squinted hard to see the hands properly—read quarter past six as Frost stopped again. The sun was already so low, long shadows from the trees across the river beside which he stood etched criss-cross lines, as if for a gigantic and rather lopsided game of celestial tic-tac-toe.

He felt the corners of his mouth downturning as he stared across the water. "Crocs," he murmured, and soon at sundown, other beasts of the jungle would be coming down to the water—hungry perhaps. The river could not be swum, he determined—it would be suicide.

The path of the men he was following—the terrorists he had killed had apparently been following them as well—had run to the river, then stopped. Frost checked the ground by the water line, finding the flat, smooth impression of what seemed to be a rubber raft. He cursed softly under his breath. To follow them now, he would need a craft with which to cross the river. And the only way to get such a craft was to build it. . . .

The sunlight during the daytime was stronger along the banks of the river—so more young trees grew near there, and these were the trees Frost searched for and—laboriously because his best tool was a machete—cut. He stuck to the softer wood trees as best he could, looking for trees no more than six to eight inches in diameter. He worked through into the darkness, using the flashlights of the terrorists he had killed, the exertion causing his vision to deteriorate even more. His hands were past blistering—they bled. Seven of the trees, finally pulled side by side, along the muddy embankment, together formed a wide, rough "plank" not really a raft; and using fire now he burned off the excess length, packing the wet mud over the boundary line where he wanted to preserve the logs, fanning the flames with his tattered once-white suitcoat, then as the flames leaped toward the portions of the logs he wished to save, hurling mud with his raw, still bleeding hands, onto the flames.

He smiled once during the night; he'd been afraid to sleep, lest he awaken blinded. A glance at the Rolex—two thirty A.M.—made him realize the sleep would not come. Using the battered machete, he finished trimming the small diameter logs to size; then beginning with the vine rope he'd made, finding more vines and hacking them free, he knotted the logs together, to form the raft.

Done—the Rolex was progressively harder to read—it was nearly six. He rested in the most profitable way he could, awaiting the light. Taking some of the reasonably potable water he'd stolen from the bodies of the terrorists, he soaked his hands, the pain at first worse, then the water doing at least a little to soothe them.

The machete was useless. He eyed it once in the graying dawn. After a time, when he judged the light sufficient, he clambered to his feet, his back stiff, aching, his hands swollen and the fingers

24

slightly stiff—the stiffness would go away with use.

He could barely distinguish breaks in the leaves now, and to see the far river bank above a cloudy blur was impossible. Frost looked at the machete—like an old comrade—and tossed it down, glancing once more at the twisted shape stuck in the soft mud, the blade twisted and nicked beyond sharpening or any utility.

He slipped the AK-47s across his back; carrying two guns that way was awkward as he tried using his hands and arms. Bracing himself behind the seven foot long, roughly fifty inch wide raft, he pushed it off into the water. The butt of one of the AKk-47s would serve as his paddle; the gun would rust and ruin but not before he no longer needed it. If he did not find the Chapmann crew by midday, a gun would likely be useless and in the day or so it would take the rust to truly do its damage, he would be dead or in possession of another gun. Lying flat on the raft, he dug the butt of the weapon into the water; there was almost no perceptible current so the relatively minuscule paddle would do.

Half across the river, one of the crocodiles on the far bank twitched once violently and slithered into the water; another, then another of the massive reptiles slithering in after it. Frost tried paddling faster, but the raft, crossing the river and drifting slightly downstream seemed to the one-eyed man to have a mind of its own—it would not move faster.

The nearest of the three crocodiles stopped in

the water, fifty yards from the raft. Frost wondered how you could tell if a crocodile was staring at you. Frost waved at it, mentally and physically shrugging.

The crocodile started through the water, like a submarine with a snout, cutting the water, moving swiftly and straight toward the raft.

Frost pulled himself up to his knees, shifting his "paddle" to his right shoulder and feeling the water dripping from it down his torn and dirty, once-white shirt. The jacket was gone—burned when he'd tried putting out the fires in the logs.

He tried squinting his right eye to sight across the receiver. It was blurring badly. He squinted it tight, then opened it.

He couldn't see.

Frost squinted his eye again—the crocodile had to be out there, yards from him, perhaps only feet now.

He squinted his eye shut, opened it. Darkness. "No-o-o-o!" Frost screamed.

He fired the AK-47 into the water, hearing the splash, hearing a loud, thrashing sound in the water. He fired again, then again, then again and again, the weapon smelling of hot oil, the metal of the barrel and receiver hot to his touch. The gun was empty—his right finger squeezed the trigger, again and again. Nothing. Frost fumbled at his belt, found a spare magazine and dumped the old one out; he heard it splash into the river water. He rammed a fresh magazine into place up the well, worked the bolt, then fired again into the water.

The one-eyed man stopped. The other eye—the

26

right one—was totally without vision. Darkness. And the thrashing sounds in the water had stopped.

Frost reached the butt of the AK-47 into the water, paddling with it against the water.

He felt something, heard something—he sensed it, not knowing how. Frost hammered out with the butt of the rifle as the raft shuddered, hearing a noise he couldn't really identify, then the cracking and splintering of wood. One of the crocs, he thought.

He twisted the AK-47 around in his hands and fired into the water as the raft under him started to tilt hard to his right. He raised the gun through the darkness, right and left, up and down, firing until the firing stopped.

Motionless, he knelt on the raft, water splashing across his knees.

There was no sound but the river, the screeching of birds on the banks, the pounding of his heart in his chest.

It took him what he judged as five minutes before he could force himself to move his arms enough to extend the butt of the rifle toward the water; was the croc still out there—was there another one? Slowly, he dipped the rifle butt into the water, moved it, then pulled it out, dipping it in again, slightly faster this time. He could feel the raft trembling slightly under him. But maybe, Frost thought—it was just his own body trembling.

Chapter 4

Frost fell, face forward into the mud, the raft
having slammed against the riverbank, he decided.
He crawled across it, the ooze under him pushing
itself inside his half open shirt and into his sixty-
five dollar shoes. He'd abandoned one of the
AK-47s as the raft hit; it had fallen from his hands
into the water.

Anxiously, angrily—terrified in darkness, Frost
grabbed the second rifle from where it was slung
across his back. It was in his right hand now as he
pushed up to his feet, extending his left hand forward, in a crouch, moving through the mud. He
counted his steps. "One—two—three—four—
five—six—se—" His hand found something
ahead of him—a tree trunk? It was rough. It was
a tree trunk. He sank into the mud beside it, on
his knees, then twisted around in the mud, placing
his back against it.

There had been crocs up and down the river
bank—they could be yards, feet, even inches from

him, he thought. He was totally blind. It wasn't like the times he'd rehearsed blindness. The blindfold would always come off. The furniture—such as there was—in the little apartment in South Bend, Indiana, was always in the same spot. If someone rang the doorbell you could always pull the blindfold off before someone noticed it and thought you were silly, before you had to explain you were only really terrified of one thing: losing the sight in the one eye you had left.

Frost had lost—he knew it. Eva Chapmann had won. He knew that too.

He set the rifle across his lap, found the Webley in the canvas holster on the stolen web belt and broke it open, feeling for a loaded cylinder with his left hand.

He snapped the break-open revolver closed, his left hand stroking the barrel.

"That or get eaten," he whispered to himself.

Frost tested it out, placing the muzzle of the revolver to his temple. That wasn't a sure way. He opened his mouth, placing the muzzle just inside. He put the gun down, murmuring, "Bess—Bess." He closed his right eye—what difference it made he couldn't notice. The one-eyed man—now blind—sat in the dark, in the mud, listening to the animal sounds. His right fist knotted around the butt of the revolver. "Not yet," he whispered. "Not yet."

He sat there in his personal darkness—he could go nowhere else.

Chapter 5

Frost remembered that the first time they'd made love, Bess had told him his fingernails were dirty—that she'd never been made love to by a man with dirt under his fingernails, but that she liked it. It had been in sort of a cave behind a small waterfall, hidden. And they'd made love there through the night and somehow everything had been different for him after that. It was the first time he'd fallen in love with somebody. Maybe the first time he'd loved anybody at all.*

Frost remembered the time in Canada, when he'd been shepherding the little genius up to his father, the grown-up genius with no time for a son. Bess's maternal instinct was a strong one and for the first time in his life, Frost had realized there was a father instinct in him—he'd saved the boy's life, saved him from nearly drowning and when Frost and Bess had finally delivered the boy

*See, They Call Me The Mercenary #1, The Killer Genesis

30

to his father. . . . There had been gunfights with terrorists, the most terrifying plane ride Frost had ever had, the whole thing with the nuclear weapon the terrs had been planning to drop. But he and Bess had handed the boy over, safely, sound, and both of them had felt the loss.*

The whole thing with Bess's presumed death, the clues that had led him nearer to her, finally her freedom, the woman back with him, beside him in his bed.

Money—the pursuit of it. He had money now, a fat enough account for him, but slender by Swiss bank standards, he knew. At least Bess would get it.

There had to be another way, Frost thought. Suicide to him had always been repugnant. He could try to walk it out. With the sun on his face if he stayed near enough the river bank to be out of the jungle shade, he could tell east from west. If he walked along the river, eventually there would be a settlement. But on which side: would he miss it completely? The crocs, the snakes, the animals that came to the water to drink. Animals could sense another animal too weak to fight, unable to defend itself.

He wondered absently how far along the river he'd drifted?

Frost thought about the gun in his hand—was there—

"I tell ya', Firth—I heard a fuckin' automatic

*See, They Call Me The Mercenary #5, Canadian Killing Ground rifle out 'ere! Now look down there by the bank and cut the gripin', will ya'? God Almighty—what a lazy bastard you are. The old Deathwitch'll have our 'eads if that one-eyed son of a bitch made it across the river! He should be blind as a bat by now.''

Frost let out a deep breath—silently and slipped his back down along the tree trunk, spreadeagling himself in the mud. The "Deathwitch" was the nickname of Eva Chapmann—Frost had always thought it was too kind.

Chapter 6

"Who you callin' bloody names, arsehole?"

Frost, slithering across the mud away from the voices and he hoped toward cover, assumed the voice belonged to Firth.

It was the first voice again. "There's bloody four of us—one of 'im—what the bloody hell you scared of, boyo?"

"He ain't gonna necessarily be too blinkin' fond of us now, is he?"

"Bite it—and get down that slope there and check out the river bank."

"There's crocs down there, Jergens; why don't you get on down there and look-see for the blighter?"

"Firth!"

"What the hell do you want—I'm ass tired with you, Jergens—who made you some bloody officer? What, you been hopping in bed with 'er highness again. I'd sooner puke."

"Watch what you say about her, you bastard or

33

I'll let ya 'ave it here and now.''

"Bullshit you will, man!"

Frost closed his eye; again it was useless. If two of them fought, he realized, the weapons' sounds would let him home in on them with his own weapons—there was a slim chance that spraying to right and left of the sound, spraying until he either got hit or ran out of ammo—it might get them all—especially if they helped.

There was a new voice. "Jergens—Firth is right; you wanna check down there with them ruddy crocs. You go on and do it yerself—shit—"

"Butt out, Cole," Jergens yelled.

"Cole's right—nobody pays 'nough to get yer bloody leg bit off now, do they? You think it's so bloody important to check the riverbank—then do it, Jergens."

A fourth voice—all four men, together.

Frost squeezed his right eye shut, concentrating on the sound.

They were above him, to his right if he turned around, came around the tree trunk.

One grenade—he had two. Make it two. Soviet grenades, but Frost remembered how to work them. He could toss one, then toss the second a minute later; then, if he wasn't dead, crawl up the embankment toward where he'd heard the sounds of the explosions, to find the bodies and kill them all. Maybe—maybe the antidote for the injection—if there was an antidote.

"Better than dying here—killing myself," Frost murmured.

"What the hell was that? I heard me a bloody

whisper out there!"

"Jergens—you old lady. If you think the bloke is out there, just go down and shoot him!"

"Firth—I ain't telling you again—"

"Got that right," Frost muttered. He tossed the first grenade, dropping to his knees behind the tree as the explosion rocked the ground under him. He could feel the dirt raining down on him, hear it.

He was counting. Thirty seconds, he decided. He tossed the second grenade, then opened up with the AK-47, spraying up, down, right and left.

The AK-47 clicked empty. Frost dumped the magazine and loaded a fresh one, on his feet beside the tree trunk—if they shot him, it was better than his own hand.

He fired the magazine out, dumping it, loading a fresh one, starting to fire again.

No sounds—no gunfire, no moans, no running feet.

Frost felt ahead of him with his left hand, walking slowly, the gun in his right hand, waving ahead of him—maybe shaking he thought, like his body shook. "Anybody?" Frost shouted. No one answered.

He tripped, grabbing the front handguard of the rifle; but it was only a root, and ahead of him the ground seemed to rise. The embankment? He started to climb up the dirt, but it was muddy there and he slipped, skidding, down, rolling. Still no one had shot. Frost started moving again, crawling on hands and knees, flattening his feet against the dirt as he started along the embankment.

His free left hand reached the top and he snaked the muzzle of the rifle across the ground ahead of him. "Anybody! Anybody?"

No sound. Frost walked, in a low crouch, feeling ahead of himself in the darkness of his blindness. He tripped. Wetness, stickiness—blood? A man's body.

He edged back, then his left hand moved across the face. Dead, eyes open and staring up. Frost crawled on hands and knees along the ground, searching for the other bodies. He found what felt like an arm, but there was no hand and the arm wasn't attached to a body.

His right knee butted into something like a large coconut, rolling across the ground. It would be a human head—Frost was almost glad he couldn't see it. He sat on the ground, listening for movement, for the slightest unnatural sound, but there was none.

Frost slung the AK-47 across his back, crawling along the ground again, finding the bits and pieces of bodies, looking for the trunks, the torsos to which backpacks and utility belts would be attached.

He couldn't judge the time properly, but it was getting hotter—near noon?

Leather feeling, but too stiff and thin for that—plastic. The size of a large, thick wallet. There was a snap closure. He opened it, folding the plastic case thing out. He felt two glass or plastic containers. They seemed the same size by feel, but one seemed lighter.

Would the injection have been pre-prepared?

Or would it have come from one of the bottles? The lighter bottle would be the one with the injection, the heavier one the antidote—maybe?

He unzipped the interior of the case— disposable hypos. He could tell by the feel. He worked one—it was empty.

Frost sat on the ground, feeling the sun, warm on him, the mud on him drying. He heard the birds back in the trees, and the sound of heavy wings overhead; the vultures for the four dead men. Blind, they would attack him soon.

Blind equalled dead under the circumstances, he knew. There was no reason to suppose there was an antidote for the drug which had caused the blindness, or even if there were, that the men carried it. It would have been wise, a precaution, but they had not sounded like wise men.

He hefted the bottles, again determined the infinitesimal difference in weight.

The sounds of the wings were louder now in the sunlit darkness that trapped him.

He fired a burst of three rounds into the air with the AK-47. The fluttering became louder now, then stopped. They would be back in minutes.

Frost took the empty hypo, opened the bottle and inserted the needle, letting it fill—he hoped—slowly. He squirted the needle upward. How much of it was needed? A full hypo? Two, less than half—he didn't know.

He found by feel the sorest of the two spots in the crook of his left elbow and rammed the needle home, depressed the plunger and sat there, a long time. He decided it was empty and he pulled the needle out and threw it away.

He couldn't pass out, or the vultures would take him for carrion. He sat there. Nothing was—he twisted forward, onto his face in the dirt, his stomach in knots, his chest tight, his head feeling like it would explode. "Dammit!" He shouted, and for a moment the noise of the vultures flapping their wings overhead even stopped. But it started again as he writhed there. Doubling over again, he loosed a burst skyward with the AK—the fluttering wouldn't stop as long this time when the birds realized he couldn't hit what he couldn't see. . . .

Chapter 7

Frost opened his right eye, his guts churning in pain and took the Webley .38 and aimed it at the head of the buzzard and fired. The bird exploded and Frost turned his face away, rasping, "You filthy—"

He tried to stand up, his stomach aching. He threw up onto the ground at his—"Ground—I can see the ground! I can see the ground! I saw that damned bird! I can see the gun—I can see my gun—Jees; I can really—"

Frost threw up again, his stomach still paining him. He walked toward the nearest tree trunk and unzipped his fly and pissed; he could even see that, he thought.

"See—"

Frost looked upward—the sky was purple. He wondered if it had ever been quite that purple before. Purple skies, green eyes for Bess, black for his eyepatch, his Browning was a dull silvery color, his white suit—he looked down at his

39

pants. Torn, bloodstained, mud-caked; they were no longer white. He didn't really care.

He moved slowly, his stomach still hurting but the pain subsiding. He bent down and found the bottles on the ground. The one he had used for the injection. He couldn't understand the chemical names on the makeshift label. The other bottle—it evidently wasn't the stuff he'd been injected with. He would have laughed, or cried—the second bottle was venom extract from the mamba snake. It would have killed him—one drop—in less than thirty seconds.

He walked toward the trees, leaning against one, not minding the buzzards now. He wheeled and ran a burst from the AK-47 into them, killing five of them before the rest took flight. He could see. And buzzards would never be one of the things he enjoyed seeing, scavenging on men, regardless of who the men had been.

He closed his eye, opened it, closed it, opened it; he could really see. "Really works," he smiled. He decided that if people had lives like a cat, he'd used all of his.

But he'd need new ones then—to find Eva Chapmann in the jungle and kill her.

Mechanically, almost, his eye surveyed the bodies on the ground. Of the two dead men semi-intact, physically one looked tall enough that his cammie fatigues wouldn't be a bad fit. And Englishmen always tried to stay clean. . . .

FN-FAL, FN Military High Power. Gerber MkII Survival Knife. C-rations—ham and lima beans were better than nothing. There was a pack of cigarettes, Pall Malls. A good friend of his smoked Pall Malls. All his Camels were gone; he'd smoke Pall Malls and be surprised when he opened the next pack of rations. The jungle boots were a little large but he put on two pairs of socks and that took care of the problem. Frost was a twelve D; the dead man whose boots he wore had to be a thirteen.

Frost shrugged; considering the donor of the boots was dead, he didn't feel at all upset he wasn't filling the man's shoes. One of the field packs had a flask in it: Scotch. He had always felt egalitarian concerning liquor—scotch, rum, bourbon, blended, vodka—if it was free, he'd drink it.

He drank from the flask, the liquor burning his throat. He drank again, and this time it didn't burn. He laughed at himself—he was reading the serial number on the FN High Power. Just because he could do it. . . .

He parted the bright green jungle foliage—they had to be Eva Chapmann's men. Most normal men who worked for a normal commander wouldn't be doing what they were doing. It was her father, Marcus Chapmann, all over. Common sense told him to leave it alone. Other things told him not to.

A black girl—a native by her dress. She was on the ground, two men holding her arms by the wrist, two more holding her legs by the ankles. A fifth man, an officer, Frost thought, was smoking a cigarette, watching. The sixth man was running his right hand over the woman's vaginal area,

41

bending over her, laughing. She was screaming.

Frost swung the binoculars back to the officer. He was using the butt of his cigarette to light a fresh one. That decided the one-eyed man. The Chapmann officer was smoking his own brand and there had been none with the C-Rations—after smoking through the small pack of Pall Malls, he'd searched everywhere through the rations; booze, no Camels. Maybe the Chapmann officer even had an extra pack—maybe a carton.

He swung the binoculars back along the ground—the woman had stopped screaming. The sixth man, tall and grubby looking with a heavy mustache, not trim, Frost thought, like his own, was dropping to his knees on the ground between the woman's legs now, his penis sticking out of his open cammie pants like a carrot in front of a mule.

Frost set down the glasses, remembering for a second the way Bess had always joked about a one-eyed man preferring binoculars.

He worked the safety on the FN-FAL and shouldered the weapon, parting a little more of the brush, then leveling the front and rear sights, lining them up, squinting over them—the man with the open pants. Frost pumped the trigger, a three-round burst of 7.62 mm NATO slugs ripping into the scruffy looking man—in the logical place too, Frost thought.

The man screamed, blood drenching the front of his pants as he rolled back across the ground. He was screaming a little, but then he died, Frost decided; the body stopped thrashing around.

Frost fired again, at the man to the girl's right, splitting the head like a melon.

The man on the girl's left was on his feet, the girl trying to twist away from the men still holding her ankles, the men themselves staring dumbly up into the brush toward Frost and the gunfire. But the man who'd loosed her left wrist was swinging a duplicate FN-FAL into action. He never made it, Frost cutting him down with a long, upsweeping burst that started just below the belt and ended at the center of the face.

The body spun like a dervish in a ritual dance, the body flopping then, like a wet pair of socks flat on the ground, not quivering.

The two ankle fetishists—Frost mentally labeled them that—were up, one of them trying to pry a pistol from his belt holster, the full flap slowing him. Frost didn't have that problem—he fired a short burst from the assault rifle into the man's chest. The man spun, the pistol finally coming out of the leather and discharging, in his twitching right hand, into the dirt at his feet as he fell.

The other ankle holder was running, the girl running too—toward Frost and the bush where he hid.

She was in his line of fire and Frost couldn't shoot. The second ankle holder had his assault rifle and fired, the girl falling to the ground. "Bastard," Frost rasped, emptying the FN's magazine into the Chapmann soldier's crotch and upper torso. The man dropped his rifle, slapping back against a tree trunk, staring at himself, then

43

slithering down its length to a heap at the ground.

The officer was running.

Frost—the FN rifle empty—snatched the High Power from the belt holster.

He started to run. The girl—she was screaming, holding her right leg—was on the ground, staring up at him. He tried to remember something in some African language that he could tell her. Instead, he smiled, then started running again.

He could hear the sound of an engine starting. Chapmann's people always like to drive, Frost remembered; never walk when you could drive.

He crossed the small clearing, hitting the tree line and bulling his way through it.

There was a wide, savanna grass clearing on the far side of the trees. There was a Land Rover there, starting to move.

Frost half ran, half dove from the trees, tripping on something, rolling, bringing up the muzzle of the High Power.

He fired once, then once again, the officer's foraging cap blowing into the wind.

He got to his feet, starting to run, starting to fire again, but the Land Rover was drifting into a lazy circle and Frost stopped, his heart pounding in his chest, sweat streaming down his face and back and arms. The Eva Chapmann officer was dead, head against the wheel, the horn sounding, blaring, the foot apparently locked on the accelerator as the Rover cut its arc.

Frost watched it for too long a time, he thought, then started to run, getting up alongside on the passenger side, climbing aboard and

44

booting the dead man out into the tall savanna grass, depressed and matted down now from the circling tire treads.

Frost let the accelerator ease up, but didn't brake. He let the vehicle slow and stared ahead of him, then braked quickly.

He jumped out. The Chapmann officer was definitely dead. There would be maps, papers, things like that. But there was the black girl they'd been about to rape. Frost decided her leg wound was more pressing.

As he started across the savanna, he looked back at the dead body a moment. Eva Chapmann had done one thing for him, Frost smiled—given him the feeling of *deja vu*. And he had been there before.

Chapter 8

The black girl didn't speak English very well, but then again, the one-eyed man reminded himself, he was no Shakespeare.

"What's your name?" Frost found himself shouting, like most people do when trying to speak with someone they anticipate doesn't speak English well. If you shout, it somehow makes the speaker feel his words will mystically become understandable. Frost lowered his voice and tried again. "What is your name, girl?"

"Elizabeth—what yours, man?"

Frost looked up into her dark eyes and smiled. "I'm sorry. That's the best I can do on the leg—it'll hurt, but the bullets went through at least. You need a hospital."

The girl winced as Frost closed the bandage and secured it. "I know a doctor—a place."

"Where?"

"You take me—maybe?"

"Yeah," Frost smiled. "I take you—maybe.

How old are you?''

"Sixteen—"

"I just hope your father doesn't catch me—I wouldn't want to get him upset or anything."

She laughed.

"What's so funny?"

"He the village chief—he get mad, you in big trouble," and she gestured with her hands, like a fisherman describing the length of his catch.

"Chief—you people have guns—you know—fight the terrs?"

"Guns—some."

"Would your daddy do me a favor?"

"He will give you anything—you save my life. I am worth—"

"Don't tell me six cows," Frost laughed.

"He would give me—to you," she smiled again.

"I've already got one girl and I've been trying to taper off—but thanks anyway," Frost smiled.

"You no like black girls—African?"

"Ohh—yeah, listen; I'm not pre—not against anything like that. But sixteen? That I'm against. If we bump into each other again in about eight or ten years, look me up, huh?"

"I look you up—" she laughed.

Frost started to help her to her feet, then she screamed and started to pass out. "Leg—aww—" she shouted.

"Leg—ohh," Frost mimicked badly. "Okay; want a pony back ride?"

"Pony? Pony?" she said over and over again.

"Elizabeth—ride on my back to the Land Rover—go for a drive—find your village or a hospital—huh?"

"Elizabeth ride your back—ha!"

Frost looked into the girl's eyes. Like teenagers everywhere, he thought—weird.

He stooped over and let her climb aboard. "You carry my gun—rifle—right?"

"Elizabeth carry," she laughed and Frost, trying to stand semi-erect under her weight on his back, handed her up his FN-FAL. This time, it wasn't so easy crossing the tree cover into the savanna. "Elizabeth like you, man."

Frost grinned up at her, already out of breath—she was heavier than she looked. "Wonderful—wonderful, Elizabeth," Frost told her. . . .

Elizabeth, despite her constant giggling and bizarre English, gave good directions, Frost decided. He gathered from what she said that she had been taken from the stream near her village by the Eva Chapmann men, hauled off through the jungle and been elected the afternoon's recreation. The village was twenty miles, from the way the girl talked, and the village was the place where the hospital or doctor was—Frost wasn't quite sure which from the way she talked. At least he thought that was what she meant.

"Elizabeth—why did the men take you—I mean—why your village?" Frost half shouted over the engine noise; he decided the Rover needed a new muffler.

"Kill two, three maybe; run off. Lotta girl get took from village by terrs maybe, maybe like them crazy white mans."

"What do your people do about it?" he asked her, saying the words slowly.

"Hunt terrs, hunt crazy white mans—sometime find bodies, never find terrs or white mans; all girls all dead."

Frost looked at her, then shook his head. The typical Chapmann native policy: kill, rape, steal, mutilate. "Like father like daughter," Frost muttered to himself.

"What Frosty say?"

"Not Frosty, dammit—Frost—Frost. F R O S T—not Frosty—"

"Not Frosty—okay," she laughed.

Frost wondered if one of the wild shots had maybe hit her in the head.

The way she guided him, Frost decided, was certainly no road. There was sparse savanna grass and the ground seemed to be rising out of the jungle, but the going was slow; a broken axle even at the thinning edges of the jungle means throw away the vehicle.

She was talking, chattering, keeping up a steady flow of incomplete sentences, split infinitives and malapropisms; Frost decided finally it was the way the girl evidenced her hysteria over what had happened. Otherwise she had been too impossibly calm.

Frost stopped the Rover on a low rise and watched where Elizabeth's finger pointed.

"There—there!"

Some thatched huts, three pre-fab metal buildings and a larger low, flat-roofed building looking to be made of logs. There were some naked children playing in what was either the central square or main street, and as Frost threw the Rover into gear and bounced it down the rise and along a gradual defile toward the center of the village, the children began to scream and run.

Frost slowed the Rover, the speedometer hovering just under ten miles per hour as he started the vehicle into the village.

The children had vanished, but adult males were appearing. The weapons they carried were a bizarre, motley collection of long guns—long tubed, double barrel shotguns, FN-FALs, bolt action British Lee-Enfields, even one M-16 he spotted. A tallish man, bigger by a head at least than the others, strode from the long, low, log hut with the thatched flat roof. There was a peculiar looking long gun held at a sort of high port in his hands.

Frost pumped the Land Rover's brakes and it screeched to a halt, the armed men of the village ringing themselves around Frost, the girl and the vehicle. Frost studied the taller man, watched him walking forward, toward Elizabeth's side of the Land Rover. The gun the man carried was a drilling; two shotgun barrels with a rifle barrel underneath. At least at the distance, the gun looked in pristine condition.

"Who you be, man?"

It was the tall man, his black eyes staring squarely at Frost.

The girl was saying something in a language Frost vaguely thought familiar but couldn't understand. The man said something to her, then the girl responded—again, Frost could not understand a word.

The tall man waved his drilling in the air and shouted something. Suddenly, the men ringing the Land Rover were reaching for Frost. Frost started for the FN-FAL, then gave up on it, grabbing for the High Power in the holster at his belt. But the hands of the men around the Rover were dragging him out of the vehicle, hands on his arms, almost pinning them, hands on his legs and thighs, hands going under him.

He was sprawling, but across the upraised hands of the men of the village. A short, skin and bones looking older man reached out toward Frost who tried to block the man's hands, but the left hand got past him. Frost could feel it patting him on the back. The faces of the men holding him up in the air were laughing faces, smiling. Suddenly—Frost recognized the voice as it boomed; the tall man shouted again and Frost was set gently down on his feet before the man. Someone handed Frost back his rifle.

"Elizabeth my daughter—very much thank you." The tall man extended his right hand and smiled. Frost took it.

Chapter 9

Elizabeth's father was the chief of the village, or the headman, or whatever he was called. That much was obvious, Frost decided, as he followed the big man—called Mbobo—through the wooden front door of the log structure and inside. The floor was wood, flat smooth boards that had obviously been cut at a saw mill and not by native craftsmen. Inside the log house was a table, huge like something one would expect for a dinner party or a board meeting, Frost decided. Twelve chairs were at the table. Beyond it, everything appeared to be standard living quarters. There was a large radio with a crank operated generator beside it, cupboards holding food and plates and at the extreme far end, several beds. Not a bad place, actually, Frost thought.

"Sit down, man; tell you name," and Mbobo sat at the head of the long table, Frost sitting down at Mbobo's right. The girl—Elizabeth, an older woman hovering around her now—lay on a couch like bed, a mustard colored liquid being poured on her leg wound.

"Frost; not Frosty like your daughter says," Frost smiled.

"Frost—strong sounding word for name. You save my daughter, Elizabeth, kill many of Deathwitch men. Whatever you wish—it yours," and the man extended his hands expansively around the room, then smiled.

Frost looked around the room, then looked back at Mbobo. "Thank you; but seeing how happy you are to get your daughter back is thanks enough."

The tallish man barked something to the older woman, the woman—Elizabeth's mother? —started across to the far side of the structure. "Eat with me; we talk."

Frost nodded; the food looked like pretty standard canned goods and he was tired of C-rations. Frost took one of the pilfered Camels from the breast pocket of his pilfered cammie fatigue blouse and lit it with the blue yellow flame of his battered Zippo. The flame was getting low.

"Lighter fluid?" Without waiting for Frost to say anything, the man called out across the room. In less than a minute, Elizabeth's mother was coming back with a small blue and yellow can. Frost took the can and smiled, pulling the guts out of the Zippo and inspecting the can, trying to decipher how it opened. As Frost began to fill the lighter, Mbobo asked, "Why did this thing? Save Elizabeth?"

"Well—seemed like a good idea at the time.

I'm not fond of Eva Chapmann—the Deathwitch like you called her. She tried to kill me. That's why I'm here."

"Tell me—food here in little bit. Tell me."

Frost nodded. He needed to tell it to somebody. He recounted his abduction from the hotel, his awakening in the jungle with the needle marks in his arm, his desperate attempt to track Eva Chapmann's men through the jungle. He left out killing the Communist terrorists, not knowing where Mbobo's sympathies were.

The food was canned pork and beans and meat that tasted like steak—he didn't ask. It tasted good and that was enough. Finishing his second plate, Mbobo interrupted him, saying, "This Deathwitch should die."

"I go along with ya there, my friend. And she's gonna die."

"One man—crazy. Many men—maybe."

Frost looked across his forkful of beans and studied Mbobo's face. The man was in his middle thirties, if that, a high forehead, wide apart eyes and teeth that against the blackness of the face seemed radioluminescent in their brightness. "Many men?" Frost finally echoed.

"Elizabeth safe—eight other girls like Elizabeth dead. Government military fight the terrs—no time to fight men who kill our girls. Are you soldier?"

"Sometimes," Frost smiled.

"Be general—we all kill Deathwitch together."

Frost just looked at the man a moment. "Together?"

"Together—right word?"

"Right word," Frost nodded. "Together . . . How many men with guns?"

Mbobo thought a moment, then shouted to Elizabeth. She answered. "My father no good English numbers. I very good English everything. Ten plus eight we got."

"Eighteen?" Frost looked at Mbobo.

Mbobo looked at Elizabeth and she echoed, "Ten plus eight we got."

"Eighteeth," Mbobo smiled.

"Eighteen," Frost corrected. "You wanna come kill Eva—the Deathwitch with me?"

"Very good thing—okay?"

Frost lit another Camel. "Very good thing," he repeated. "Okay."

Chapter 10

There were nineteen men counting Elizabeth's father, Mbobo, twenty when Frost counted himself. There had been other, younger men who could have gone. But Frost had insisted and Mbobo agreed that the village should not be left unguarded. The guns Frost had collected from the Chapmann men he'd killed rescuing Elizabeth he'd given to Mbobo. Some of the eighteen men had rearmed themselves and left their old guns with the village defenders. So two of the bolt action Lee Enfields had disappeared and one double barreled shotgun. Frost had given Mbobo two pistols—two more FN High Powers, keeping two for himself and dispersing the others. He had taken the pistols from the original Chapmann band he'd encountered where he'd first re-equipped.

Mbobo now, a holstered High Power on each hip, the one on his left hip, butt forward, and his German made drilling in his hands, called the column to a halt. The chantlike singing stopped too. There had been more jungle to cross and now, above them, as Frost wiped his right forearm across his sweat drenched forehead, he could see the mountains. "Map, they give bad map—goes through worst part of jungle. Take five days for healthy man run fast. Better way here. Up mountain, down mountain—high flat place tall grass. There." Mbobo pointed toward a high peak and Frost nodded. Muscles he hadn't used in so long he'd forgotten them ached. He studied his hands for a moment. Elizabeth's mother had put something on the raw blisters and they were already starting to heal, apparently the same medication put on Elizabeth's leg. The one-eyed man shook his head, smiling. He decided that someday medical science would become sophisticated enough to experiment with all the things so-called primitive people had used for thousands, perhaps millions of years.

Mbobo, ceremoniously, shouted to his men, "Take five!"

Frost looked at Mbobo, looked away then looked back. "Take five?"

"Radio—good talk," Mbobo declared. . . .

Frost shouldered into the rain poncho he'd taken from one of the Chapmann men; it was the closest thing he had to a coat and as they climbed the mountain, the temperature began to drop quickly. A stiff, cold wind blew laterally across the trail as they stopped again. "How much farther?"

"Up and down," Mbobo said cheerfully.

"Deathwitch has many guns—" Frost stopped, shaking his head. He was starting to sound like Mbobo and Elizabeth. He smiled, thinking about the girl. As they'd left the village, the women and children and older people out to bid them farewell, Elizabeth had limped from her father's house, the mustard colored liquid solidified in streaks over the wounded area. She had reached up to Frost and kissed him on the cheek. Frost had bent down to her and kissed her forehead.

Frost began again, Mbobo looking puzzled. "The Deathwitch—she has lots of guns, probably electronic intruder detection systems. Sentry dogs too, I think. We've gotta start being careful now, to avoid detection as long as possible."

"I there once—followed men who killed one of girls. I show you way right up to front door."

Frost looked at the man, shaking his head, saying, "What? That's—"

"Built for white men, built for terrs, not built for Mbobo. Mbobo knows. Built house with many men village—many years."

"You helped build the house for Marcus Chapmann?"

"Big Colonel ran whole province those day—him say build me house, we build house."

"But—"

"Chapmann cheap."

"What?"

"Cheap—dry stream, fill with little stones, rain comes and go way."

"What?" Frost repeated.

"Little stones go, put in more little stones.

58

Little stones cut stream when go way—big hole. Mbobo show Frost."

"Mbobo show Frost," the one-eyed man repeated. He could hardly wait. . . .

Six hours march out of the mountains—two P.M. on the black face of the Rolex Frost wore—had brought them in sight of the high plateau and the house that dominated its center. Chapmann had always had a passion for walled, castle-like structures, Frost remembered, and this was typical of him. A broad, low, Mediterranean style house with a tiled roof—the tiles flown in? Generous grounds and then a high, stone and mortar wall surrounding house and grounds.

"There—see!"

Mbobo was pointing toward the far corner of the wall nearest them and Frost parted the savanna grass in front of him again and stared through the right tube of his binoculars. He didn't see anything. He adjusted the focus. A small stream bed, angling down from the mountains, barely noticeable. Built in the dry season, just a minor depression in the ground, but in the wet season the tiny stream bed would be a raging torrent. Frost studied it as it met the very corner of the wall, where two sides of the wall joined at right angles. The entire base of the corner was shored up with gravel. "The little stones," Frost murmured to himself.

Frost put down the binoculars, turned and looked at Mbobo. "I don't understand—they've closed the hole."

"Look one more again."

Frost shook his head, then picked up the binoculars, studying the wall. The little stones cut—something like that Mbobo had said, Frost recalled. And now Frost understood. The little stones had cut the wall, over the years. Chunks of wall were pieced together where the stream bed edged against the corner. The cracks were visible, pieced together with mud or cement. A good chisel and a strong man with patience and . . .

"Frost see?"

"Frost see," the one-eyed man smiled.

They would have to wait for dark. But now instead of going over the wall, jarring the electronic security system into effect, they could go under the wall. Silently, carefully—but under it. Twenty men, himself included, into the compound, perhaps totally undetected until they were inside. The Chapmann men Frost had killed had carried grenades. That would get the attention away from the house. Frost studied the grounds through the binoculars—a hundred yard run from the wall to the patio at the side of the house. Then he could kill Eva Chapmann.

Frost looked at Mbobo and smiled, using his right forefinger like a gun barrel and pointing toward the house. "Deathwitch—bang!"

Chapter 11

Frost looked skyward. He decided then and there that were he ever to become an astronaut, he would spray paint the bright side of the moon non-reflective black, in that way rendering useless the old expression "Dark of the Moon" but also rendering it unnecessary. It was nights like this that he truly appreciated it. The moon was ridiculously bright, the stars out of its aura crystal clear. On impulse, he glanced down to the FN-FAL in his hands. He could read the serial number. "Shit!"

"What Frost say?"

Frost looked at Mbobo, saying, "Nothing of consequence. I was just wishing for a darker sky. If anyone looks over that wall, they'll spot us."

"For sure," Mbobo agreed.

"You could have at least disagreed with me," the one-eyed man murmured.

The camouflage stick rubbed on his face and the backs of his hands itched. He had taped everyone's sling swivels for them, jokingly—but Mbobo had taken it that way too—advised the chief to keep his lips tight together. Mbobo had smiled at that and in the moonlight against Mbobo's black skin, had Frost had a mirror then the man would have seen the rationale for the advice.

They had stopped the belly crawl up the dry stream bed a moment earlier. Mbobo had evidently heard something and signalled the stop himself. Frost had heard nothing. But now Mbobo gave the signal to go on and Mbobo's eighteen impromptu "warriors," Mbobo and Frost himself once more began wriggling along the stream bed. The wall was perhaps a hundred yards distant from Frost, three of Mbobo's men some seventy-five yards ahead, armed with makeshift chisels . . .

Frost reached the wall alongside Mbobo, flattening himself against it, his eye alternately riveted to the top of the wall and to the men near his feet, prying out the huge sections of stone and mortar as though they were children's building blocks.

There was a loud—at least to Frost—scratching noise and Frost looked down. The last of the blocks was moved. Frost looked into Mbobo's face.

"Ready now," Mbobo rasped.

"Ready now," Frost answered.

Frost ducked down, peering through the chink in the wall. Because of the bright moonlight he could see clearly across the grounds. A man with a sentry dog was walking from the far end of the house, more than two hundred yards away.

There was no one else in sight; Frost presumed they would be on the wall near the gates and in the far end of the house, the Deathwitch's men. The name had a strange ring to it, Frost thought; but it was too kind a name for her, he decided once again.

Were the men with him a company of trained Special Forces men, commandos, men experienced in the kind of work needed, Frost thought—he looked beside him. Mbobo, using hand and arm signals, was dispatching the men, the first of them starting through the niche in the wall.

Frost looked at the African.

Mbobo smiled—the teeth like a luminous dial on an alarm clock. "Me fix," the man smiled.

Mbobo was starting through the niche. Frost shrugged and followed behind him.

He wondered earlier at the bow—now he saw its purpose. The skinny, older man, the one who'd slapped Frost on the back in the village square, had the bow taut now, one arrow notched in place, the second in his left hand beside the prod of the bow.

There was a hissing, almost whistling sound as the first arrow took flight, a soft yelp from the sentry dog as it dropped in its tracks, still better than a hundred and fifty yards off. Almost instantly the bow drew back again, the second arrow taking flight. The shadowy figure of the dog handler went down.

Frost started to move, slapping the old man on the back and smiling. "Hot damn," the one-eyed man rasped.

Frost broke into a run, hugging the wall. He heard a muted scream above him, then the unmistakable thudding sound of a body dropping. It had to be Mbobo's men—Eva Chapmann's men would have used a gun to respond to attack.

Frost stopped in his tracks, glancing behind him. Mbobo was there, gesturing into the darkness. Frost nodded, seeing the shape too, standing beside a small fountain, a man staring up at the top of the wall.

Mbobo started to move, Frost holding the man by the arm, stopping him.

Frost handed his FN-FAL to Mbobo, then withdrew the big Gerber from the sheath on his belt, biting down on the double edged knife as he placed it between his teeth, biting down hard to keep it from edging back in his mouth and cutting the sides of his mouth. He dropped into a crouch and ducked into the deeper shadow from the wall as he started toward the fountain. He froze, waiting, the man turning around, but not seeing him. The man shouldered an assault rifle and started away from the fountain.

Frost broke into a dead run.

The sentry started to turn.

Frost sprang, his left hand going out for the sentry's throat, his legs wrapping around the man's torso, the body sagging beneath him. Frost's right hand snatched for the big spear point in his teeth. He hammered it diagonally into the left side of the man's neck.

The man's eyes opened wide, and Frost could

feel the lips moving under his left hand as he clamped the mouth shut. He pulled out the knife and stabbed it in again, the movement stopping.

Frost mechanically wiped the blade clean of blood on the man's clothes as he started to his feet.

There was a noise in the air above him and Frost, dropping to his knees, then flattening himself along the ground beside the fountain looked up—aircraft landing lights, two sets, one at higher altitude than the other. He could see the silhouettes of the small planes clearly now.

"She'll get away," Frost rasped through his teeth. He pushed himself to his feet, snatched one of the G.I. style fragmentation grenades from his belt and pulled the safety clip by the pull ring. "Mbobo! Start shooting," he shouted. He released the "spoon," counting to five then lobbing the grenade into the courtyard. Before the grenade went off, he started shooting toward the top of the wall. He could feel the ground tremble under his feet, hear the roar of the grenade as it exploded, hear the tinkling of broken glass, but then the roar of his FN-FAL drowned it out and he started running.

There was gunfire all about him now, gunfire and screams from the top of the wall.

Frost glanced behind him; Mbobo was running, but stopped, shouldering the drilling and firing one of the shotgun barrels. It sounded like a ten gauge, the muzzle virtually exploding at three men charging toward him, the men withering under it, falling into heaps on the ground.

Frost started running again, into the patio, toward the doors leading into the house.

He squinted his eye shut against the brightness as floodlights clicked on with a loud hum. There was a machinegun on the roof; Frost could see tracer rounds from it as he dove behind a stone bench, the bench disintegrating under the impact of the slugs.

He pulled one of the grenades, yanked the safety pin and tossed it toward the rooftop machinegun emplacement, snatching at another grenade, pulling the ring, holding the grenade in his right fist until the time ran out, then tossing it after the first. The first grenade went off, the machinegun still firing. Almost immediately after it, the second grenade exploded and the machinegun stopped.

Frost pushed to his feet, jumped the shattered bench and ran for the patio doors. He jumped a dead body by the doors, stopped, stepped back and smashed his combat booted right foot into the glass where the two doors joined, the doors shattering inward. He fired the FN-FAL—a long burst into the room beyond the shattered doors. He dove inward, the doors shattering the rest of the way, glass streaming down on him as he rolled across the carpeted floor, up onto his knees, firing the assault rifle through the wooden doors at the far end of the room

The doors sprang inward, splintering, a man with a submachinegun falling through them. Frost was on his feet again, running. Beyond the doors was a wide, low ceilinged hall, three steps leading from it into what was apparently a living room. He ran the length of the hallway, wheeling, the FN barking in his hands, spitting fire up the stairway to the second floor. But Mbobo was there, at the base of the stairs, loosing another blast from the drilling's shotgun barrels, a man and a woman, both armed with pistols, rolling down the stairs toward Mbobo's feet.

Frost started running again for the living room, jumping the three steps, losing his balance and skidding across the smooth tiled floor on his knees. Three men were rushing out of a small door from a side room, one with a pistol, two with assault rifles. Frost fired out the FN-FAL, cutting down the two men with the assault rifles.

He made to fire a burst at the man with the pistol, but the FN clicked empty and the man dove behind the couch.

Frost dropped the rifle from his hands, snatching at the High Powers on his belt, both 9mm in his fists as he dove behind the glass-topped display case beside him.

The glass shattered. Frost looked up—the case was filled with human skulls.

Frost fired both of the High Powers, two shot bursts from each, jumped up and over the shattered display case, tripping, rolling onto the floor as the man behind the couch popped up, firing his pistol. Frost finished the roll, bullets impacting against the tiled floor inches from his head as he fired his own pistols. Frost's slugs slammed home, the man's chest seeming to twitch, lurch, then the body falling forward, collapsing across the back of the couch, the couch falling backwards under the weight.

Frost got to his feet, ramming the High Power pistols into their holsters, snatching up his FN-FAL from the floor. Mbobo was coming down the steps into the room. Frost looked at the African, saying, "You take your men upstairs; I'll grab a couple of your guys and mop up what I can out in the yard. Then I'm heading out to where those planes were coming in. If they still land, Eva Chapmann's gonna be heading for one. Use those grenades—stuff 'em down the toilets, put 'em in the oven in the kitchen—turn on the gas—be creative."

Mbobo was smiling.

Frost wheeled, starting to run toward the front door of the house. He spotted the skinny old man with the bow and arrows and shouted to him, knowing the man spoke English. "Get three men—bring 'em after me into the yard."

"Right Frosty," the man shouted back, then disappeared into a side room.

"Frosty!" the one-eyed man snarled. He kicked out the door and loosed a long burst through the open doors from the FN-FAL in his fists.

Chapter 12

Frost, the FN-FAL from the dead sentry in his fists, started through the courtyard, the old bowman running after him with some of Mbobo's men. Some of Eva Chapmann's men were still firing down from the wall and Frost, running still, fired back. The old bowman—a surprisingly fast runner, Frost thought—was beside the one-eyed man, and somehow despite the noise, Frost heard the twang of the bow and whoosh of the arrow. There was a scream from the wall and one of the submachineguns died out. Frost snatched another grenade from his belt, pulling the safety pin, shouting, "Grenade to the wall," for Mbobo's men to hear. Frost tossed the grenade.

He missed, the grenade not making the top of the wall, but falling to the wall's base. As the grenade blew, he hit the dirt, rolling behind another one of the decorative fountains in the courtyard. Chunks of mortar and rock blew in the explosion, dust raining down. He pushed himself to his knees, strafing the top of the wall with his assault rifle. He could see a body fall, then a second one and the gunfire from the top of the far wall ceased.

Frost pushed himself to his feet, running toward the open gates from the courtyard.

Running, ahead of him in a ragged line across the tall grass in the moonlight, the one-eyed man counted at least a half-dozen men, firing sporadically as they streaked toward the two airplanes which had landed and waited now with revving engines on the far side of the plateau. And ahead of the half dozen or so men he could see two, possibly three other runners, one of them—at least in his mind—looking slighter than the rest. A cloud had passed in front of the moon, and as it moved away, Frost could see the first three runners clearly. One of them, the slightly built one, had blonde hair blowing in the wind.

It was Eva Chapmann.

"Chapmann!" Frost heard himself scream the word.

Frost dropped to the grass, the FN-FAL on line toward the six figures. He started firing. Some of the men stopped, turning around, shooting.

Frost heard the whooshing sound of the skinny old man's bow, heard the booming—from far behind him—of a heavy caliber rifle. It would be Mbobo firing the rifle barrel of the drilling. . . .

Two of the six men were down, and a third one went down then.

Frost pushed up to his feet, running, firing the

70

FN-FAL at the last three men.

Passing him on the right was the skinny old man, the bow in his left hand, his right hand notching an arrow.

The skinny old man stopped, fired the bow; another of Eva Chapmann's men went down.

Frost stopped running, squaring his feet under him, the assault rifle at hip level as he fired. The last two men went down.

"Chapmann!" Frost dropped the assault rifle, tossed away his hat and bent into a dead run for the planes. One of them was already starting to move, to taxi.

Frost snatched at both High Power pistols, one in each fist as he ran.

He could see Eva Chapmann, clearly now, climbing up the wing stem of the nearest plane.

Frost threw himself down to the ground, dropping the pistol in his left hand, stabbing the pistol in his right hand forward, steadying it with his left hand.

He fired the High Power once, then once again, then a rapid two-shot burst.

Eva Chapmann fell forward across the wing stem, something falling from her left hand.

Frost started to his feet. He snatched up the second High Power from the grass, running. Eva Chapmann was moving, hands reaching out to her as the aircraft started to increase its speed.

The plane was coming toward him now. He could see the fuselage door closing, Eva Chapmann inside.

Frost stopped, stood, firing both High Power

pistols, one in each hand. The plane was coming fast, near air speed he guessed.

The slide on the pistol in his right hand locked open, empty. He emptied the High Power in his left hand, then hurtled himself to the ground, the twin engine plane yards from him, its props almost invisible with speed.

The plane crossed over him, the props missing him by mere feet. The one-eyed man tucked down into the grass, the downdraft of the plane ripping at his face and hair.

On his back, he rolled into a prone position, slamming a fresh magazine up the butt of one of his pistols, working the slide release, firing the pistol one round after the other. The old bowman was crouched beside him. The bow twanged, the whooshing sound of the arrow in flight lost in the mechanical noise of the aircraft.

Frost started to his feet, the pistol in his hand empty again, the plane vanishing into the horizon.

The old bowman extended his hand, and Frost took it, stood and looked into the man's deep set eyes, the leathery face. "Thank you," Frost whispered.

Frost glanced behind him. The second plane was stopped dead on the ground, Mbobo's men around it, holding one man from the plane at gunpoint. And Mbobo was running toward Frost, looking bizarre, incongruous. Wearing bush shorts and naked from the waist up, the African chieftain was carrying an attaché case.

Chapter 13

Frost sat crosslegged under the morning sun, smoking the Camels he'd taken from one of the dead men, reading the contents of the attaché case Eva Chapmann had dropped when Frost had wounded her.

There wasn't terribly much, but what was there seemed important.

"You learn big about Deathwitch there?" Mbobo asked.

Frost smiled up at the man, the old bowman standing beside the chief too.

"Yeah, well—looks like Eva Chapmann not only had it in for me for killing her father. She blamed me as an individual and she blamed the United States—part of this is personal notes and you can read it between the lines. She's working with some guy named Creighton Dean in Florida—that's in the United States. You'd like the climate; not unlike here. But if I didn't kill her—and I couldn't have been that lucky—that's where she'll wind up. Mentions the town of Morrison. I never heard of it; maybe in central Florida. It isn't one of the towns on either of the coasts."

"What will Frost do?"

Frost smiled, lighting another cigarette. "Frost will get that sucker," and Frost pointed to the pilot tied to the landing gear of the plane a hundred yards behind him, "Frost will—I mean, I'll get him to fly me out."

"How?"

Frost patted one of the two FN pistols on his belt. "This should do it. Granted, he can threaten to crash the plane, but then he'd get killed himself. So assuming I get into South Africa without getting shot down, I'm going to have Bess—my woman," Frost explained, happily. "Going to have Bess get herself someplace safe, then I go to Morrison, Florida. If the Deathwitch is there, she'll come after me. I can't expect her people not to notice this," and Frost tugged at his eyepatch. . . .

Frost stood beside the airplane, the pilot beside him, Mbobo and the skinny old man with the bow and the others of Mbobo's men in a semi-circle, facing him. Three of Mbobo's men had been killed, four wounded, but none of the wounds critical. All of Eva Chapmann's men—except whoever had boarded the plane with her—had died. Frost didn't want to ask Mbobo how it had just happened to work out that way.

Frost reached out his right hand, taking Mbobo's hand in his. "It sounds stupid, but you ever come to the United States—well, you know. And if you ever need me, and you probably won't, well—keep that piece of paper. That man at Diablo Security usually knows how to reach me and I'm sure you could find a way of getting in touch with him."

"Good man—good man," Mbobo smiled warmly.

Frost took the hand of the old bowman, the man nodding, smiling, almost laughing. "You tough old . . ." Frost let the sentence hang, laughing. "Here," and Frost handed the old man one of his pistols. "I'll only need one of these for the pilot—plenty of magazines and ammo around. I know it's not as much fun as a bow, but have it anyway."

The old man nodded, clapping Frost on the shoulder.

Frost pushed the pilot up ahead of him, into the plane, leaning out the door for an instant and looking at Mbobo. The one-eyed man said, "And tell Elizabeth good-bye, huh?"

Frost turned to the pilot as he started into his seat, pointing the muzzle of the High Power at the man's face. "Fly me out and you go free—try anything and maybe I'll crash into the jungle but you'll wish I'd shot you in the head," and Frost gestured with the pistol below the man's belt. "Right?"

The pilot nodded and sat down behind his controls.

The one-eyed man tried to figure out what all the levers were for, the toggle switches, the gauges; he gave up and just held onto his gun.

Chapter 14

Frost, as he walked through the doorway into the office marked, "Aaron Kruger, Special Operations," was very grateful for three things. One, the pilot had had sufficient gasoline to get to South Africa. Two, South Africa was not as turned off to anti-Communist mercenaries as many other neighboring African states. Three, that Bess had filed missing person reports and gotten the police convinced he had been taken out of South Africa to begin with against his will.

"Sit down, Captain Frost," the man behind the desk snapped without looking up.

Frost shrugged, sitting down.

"I am Aaron Kruger . . . please let me just complete this report; I'll be a moment."

"Sure," Frost nodded. Kruger was short, stocky, balding and had forearm muscles that a weight lifter would have been proud of. Frost lit a Camel in the blue-yellow flame of his Zippo, inhaling the smoke, then exhaling it hard through his nostrils. His eye began automatically searching the room for an ashtray.

"I don't smoke—here," and Kruger, still without looking up slid an ashtray off the window ledge behind him and across his desk.

"Thanks," and Frost nodded again. He still hadn't seen Kruger's eyes.

Frost studied his watch. He watched five minutes go by and was into his second cigarette by the time Kruger moved. "There—got that damnable nuisance out of the way."

Frost looked up.

Kruger was starting to stand, extending his hand across the desk. Frost took it. The man's eyes were green—hard set, but somehow not angry. "I hate paperwork; you are going to cause me a lot of paperwork, but it's not your fault. I had my men who met you at the airport contact Miss Stallman at your hotel. I asked that she spare herself the inconvenience of waiting down here for you. I promised you'd be home to her soon. A lovely woman."

"Thank you," Frost said.

"She was gravely concerned for you. Frankly, I had given you up for dead."

"Me too for a while," Frost said.

"Quite—so I understand the Deathwitch—"

"Wait—everybody uses that, Mbobo—"

"Mbobo?"

"A man who helped me—good man."

"They call Eva Chapmann the Deathwitch because of her peculiar hobby. My men tell me you had the rare opportunity of seeing her house.

77

Then you know she collects human skulls."

"That was—"

"Hers? Yes. Marcus Chapmann, whom I understand you knew, was bizarre, but in a calculating sense. I believe he was sane. I met Marcus Chapmann on one occasion years ago—before you killed him."

Frost moved in his seat but didn't say anything.

Kruger smiled. "Don't worry—I checked you out once Miss Stallman reported you missing. There was no love lost between Colonel Chapmann and myself. My only regret is that you didn't finish him off years earlier before he fathered Eva. She is the one I wish someone would eliminate. She gives all African whites a bad name. She kills because she loves it. She'll destroy anything in her way—a fine lady I'm sure you'll agree, Captain."

"Yes," Frost sighed.

"There will be forms for you to fill out. I realize you are tired; I'll put one of the secretaries in with you to help you. Then, after that, a medical—must check you for ticks—there's been an outbreak among farm animals of—"

"I haven't been near any farm animals," Frost interrupted.

Kruger smiled again. "Good; then you won't mind the medical. After that, you'll be free to go. I'll have to insist on your continued residence in our city for the next day or two—likely some questions, more forms and paperwork. I understand she escaped you but appeared wounded."

"Yes," Frost answered.

"You will endeavor to track her down in—" and Kruger looked at a note pad on his blotter, "in Florida?"

"Yes."

"What about Miss Stallman; I shouldn't think she'll be safe now."

"I'll get her to London; there's a cop I know up there who's with their Special Flying Squad who has a kind of paternal interest in her. He'll look out for her."

"Excellent. Well," and Kruger stood up from behind his desk, extending his hand again. Frost took it. "I don't think we'll see each other again, Captain. Good luck—and if you shoot the Deathwitch?"

Frost just looked at the man.

"Well—put an extra slug into her for me, hmm?"

"Sure thing."

Chapter 15

Frost didn't have a key. He nodded to Kruger's policemen who'd stationed themselves near the elevator and apparently planned to stay near him until he was out of the country. Though he didn't think they'd stop a determined Eva Chapmann, at least if they made some noise when they died, it would give him some warning.

Because he had no key, Frost knocked on the hotel door.

He started to knock again, but the door opened.

"Bess," he whispered.

She threw her arms around his neck and held him, crying. "Frost—damn it! Thank God you're alive."

Frost looked at her, her green eyes, the blonde hair down past her shoulders. She was wearing an ankle length robe and as he started to kiss her, she pulled open the tie on the robe, his hands slipping under it, across her body, the warmth of her flesh under his fingers. . . .

She was sitting cross-legged on the bed, the robe wound around her. Frost stood naked in the doorway of the bathroom, drying his hair with a towel. "Gimme that, Frost."

He tossed her the towel and she began rubbing her own wet hair with it. They'd made love fast on the bed, then after a time showered together. Frost looked at his watch. It was nearly midnight. "You sure the restaurant will be open?"

"I just called the desk; they said it doesn't close—we can get a sandwich. But room service stops at eleven during the week."

"What day is it?"

"Monday; in a few minutes it'll be Tuesday."

"I should be able to get out of here by Wednesday night—make it Stateside and down to Florida by Friday if I rush it."

"You've gotta get your guns first from Deacon."

"Maybe it's illegal, but I'll have him meet me with them at the airport in Chicago. I don't think it is, though. Then I'll fly back down to Florida. Rent a car in Miami maybe, go to Morrison, wherever that is. You give the desk that wire to Mike O'Hara yet?"

"Um-hmm—when I checked on room service just a minute ago. They said he'll get it by tomorrow. You think O'Hara will help you?"

"If he can—at least cut down on my leg work."

"Can't I go with you?"

"What if something happens—and if you're safe at least, Eva Chapmann can't try putting the

81

bag on you to get to me. I've gotta go alone. You know it."

"When will this all end, Frost—I mean, all this? When can we?—"

"Get married? Soon—I hope. We'd never be safe with Eva Chapmann out there. Before, it was because I killed her father. Now, I killed her father, destroyed her house, wounded her—I don't know how bad. She'll be after me. She's got something cooking Stateside. I don't know what. But after that, she'll come right back to me."

"Did you really almost kill yourself?"

"Yes—stone blind in the jungle isn't—"

"And you thought about me—and you didn't, ahh—"

"I thought about you and decided to sweat it out a little longer," Frost told her.

"Are you that hungry—I mean. What about a big breakfast, Frost?"

The one-eyed man reached into the bathroom and cut the light off, then walked across the room toward her.

She reached across the bed and turned off the lamp beside the telephone, her robe opening as she did. Frost eased down beside her on the still unmade bed. As he leaned her back, he could hear her whispering something. "What?"

"I said," Bess murmured, "I'll lie down on the wet spot now, but we keep the next one on your side of the bed too—agreed?"

"Then I get to sleep on the wet spot?"

"Um-hmm," she whispered, Frost tracing his fingers across the nipples of her breasts.

82

"How come?"

"You make it—you sleep in it."

"You gonna be that way after we're married?"

"Umm—probably," she murmured.

"What are you doing?"

"I'm learning how you feel in the dark—so I can—"

"Ouch—not there!" Frost snapped.

"How about there?" she whispered to him.

"There's fine," Frost answered, feeling her breath against his cheek, feeling her hands massaging at his crotch.

"Ohhh—my goodness—you really didn't want a sandwich," she laughed.

Frost could feel himself coming erect in her hands. He slipped between her thighs, her legs warm as he guided himself into her.

It felt to him as if she were pulling him, deeper and deeper into her. "It's a good thing we know each other so well and all."

"Why?" he asked her.

"Well—practice makes perfect, Frost."

He could feel her moving under him, her back arched, his left hand under it, his right hand on her left breast. She screamed a little as Frost's body trembled and he sank against her. She was right he decided; practice did make perfect.

Chapter 16

"You're gonna have to check these in as firearms at the desk."

"I know that," Frost told Andy Deacon impatiently, looking at the taller, lean man, taking the gray plastic attaché style gun case from him.

"Why didn't you just—"

"What—go after Eva Chapmann empty handed?"

"No—report her to the—"

"You didn't hear from O'Hara—the FBI guy?"

"They are not FBI guys; remember I used to be in the Bureau. Special Agents."

Frost felt stupid arguing with Deacon in the middle of the Chicago airport. "All right, Special Agent O'Hara—did you hear from him?"

"No, I would have told you. You realize how far it is from South Bend to here?"

"You run the desk at Diablo, Andy; it was legal, I think, for you to bring the guns to me since I work for you and have my Indiana permit through you."

"Still, I'm a busy—"

"Bullshit. If you were that busy you'd be trying to get me in on it."

"Well, we should have a couple of big jobs coming up. One with an—"

"Don't tell me," Frost told Deacon. "You know I'll help if I can. I don't wanna, but I will. But now I've got bigger fish to fry—Eva Chapmann."

"What the hell is a woman like that doing in the United States—a mercenary?"

"I'm a mercenary. Remember?" Frost asked brightly.

"Yeah, but—well, you're American!"

"So—maybe she's American. She was raised in Germany, but maybe she's got a U.S. passport. What difference does it make?"

"But what's she doing here?"

Frost looked at his watch. It was still on South African time. He reminded himself to reset the Rolex. He looked at Deacon. "I gotta catch a plane. Couldn't get one through to Miami. Going to Atlanta—Morrison is about equal distance between Miami and Atlanta anyway. And as soon as I find out what Eva Chapmann's up to, I'll let you know."

"When will I—"

"When I let you know; I'll be busy 'til then," Frost smiled. He stuck out his right hand to Deacon. "Andy, what can I say? They don't make guys like you anymore."

Deacon smiled at that, looking, Frost thought,

genuinely happy. Frost didn't verbalize the fact that he was happy they didn't—make guys like Deacon anymore. . . .

Frost walked rather than taking the subway style trains from the boarding area into the Hartsfield Terminal. He decided the drive between Atlanta—even south Atlanta—to Morrison, Florida would be long enough. The exercise would do him good now. Besides, he didn't like subways. They reminded him too much of elevators. . . .

The rented car had gotten a flat fifty miles outside of Morrison, Florida and Frost, exhausted, tired, had changed the flat and driven on.

It was a small town, but he decided it seemed larger early in the morning; no one was on the streets. Several of the motels he passed had signs reading "Vacancy" but only one place had a sign reading, "Hotel" instead of motel. He decided on that for the night. Frost parked the car in a vacant slot by the main entrance and walked inside. A young woman was behind the desk, looking tired.

Frost walked up to her. "I know how you feel; I'm bushed too. Got a room?"

"Yes, sir—unless you don't like waterbeds. The only two vacancies have waterbeds."

"I could sleep on a bed of nails—a waterbed'll be fine," Frost smiled.

Frost listed Diablo Protective Services as his employer on the registration, checked the metal car key ring for the license number on his car and signed his name. "Can I leave the car outside there?" and Frost pointed out the door.

"Yes, sir. That'll be fine."

"Thanks."

"Your room is the fourth one down, turn right out of the doors here. On the first floor off the parking lot."

"Gotchya," he smiled.

He pocketed the key and went through the double door, stopping by the rental car. He already had the Metalifed High Power under his jacket, but he needed his luggage and his other gun, the Interdynamics KG-9. He got the things from the car and locked it, then hiked toward his room. . . .

The room was small, but not too small, the bathroom all the way at the back, a single, huge waterbed dominating the room, opposite the footboard a dresser or desk and above that on the wall a television set.

Frost locked his door, slipped a chair under it just in case Eva Chapmann was already onto him. If someone broke down the door, the chair breaking would rouse him from the soundest sleep.

The one-eyed man kicked off his sixty-five dollar shoes; the pair he'd started out with in Africa he'd left there in the jungle. They'd been ruined anyway.

He turned on the television set. There was nothing on but code patterns.

Frost shrugged, leaning back across the bed.

"Shower—need a shower," he told himself. He hadn't showered for more than thirty-eight hours. Frost swung his legs over the side of the bed and fished in his flight bag, finding an unopened bottle of Seagrams Seven there. He opened it. Once you traveled in the South and understood the confused liquor laws, you always carried a bottle if you wanted a drink.

Frost poured a drink into a plastic cup, swallowed half of it and started to undress.

"Shower—gotta take a shower," he repeated.

Chapter 17

Frost heard the chair he'd wedged under the doorknob smash, then the sound of the security chain as it snapped away from the door frame. As he pushed open the steamed over glass shower doors, the two men with bayonet-sized knives were already halfway across the hotel room, coming for him at a run. Naked, the water streaming down over his head and body, the warm feeling in the pit of his stomach from the double shot of Seagrams before he'd stepped into the shower now instantly vanished, a cold, sick-feeling knot took its place.

The first man was about three steps ahead of the other one and charged at Frost through the open glass panels. Frost twisted the faucet all the way to "Hot" and gave the first man a shot in the face with the spray from the shower head. One leg and his knife hand were already in the shower with Frost and the one-eyed man smashed the doors closed against the killer's crotch, heard him scream. Number two was coming from the right. Frost caught his knife hand against his own right forearm on the downstroke and stepped inside to him and crossed his body with a left to the man's jaw. Frost rammed his right elbow up and forward into the man's teeth and heard the head smack back against the tiled wall as he turned back to the first man.

Number one's knife was gone, apparently on the bottom of the tub. His outstretched hands started closing around Frost's throat. Frost brought both forearms up inside the killer's arms and knocked them away. The surface of the tub was too slippery for Frost to use his feet and his hands were in a bad position for a punch, so he slapped his cupped palms over the first man's ears with full force, ramming the head back against the glass shower doors. Already, the heel of Frost's right hand was stretching out to smash at the first man's nose and drive the broken bone up into the brain to kill him. Frost started to lose his footing and his hand just connected with the man's jaw, the force of the blow driving the killer head first through the glass doors and out onto the bathroom floor.

Number two was starting to move, but the bathtub was a poor place for a fight. Frost couldn't see either of the knives in the tub because the second man's foot had blocked the drain and the soapy, bloody water was already over Frost's ankles. The one-eyed man drove the shattered shower doors hard to his right, hammering them into number two's body. Frost wanted the gun beside the bed, but that was miles away yet.

Number one, outside the tub, was starting to his feet. As Frost got out of the tub, Frost helped him along with a short knee smash to the face that drove the man's head back against the toilet bowl.

Frost's coat was closer than the gun. He got his hand to the left inside breast pocket and grabbed for the double edged boot knife there. Number one tackled him—Frost had seen him coming, out of the corner of his eye. Frost let the man start hammering on his ribs as he slipped the knife from the sheath, the double edged blade held like a dagger now in Frost's fist.

Frost elbow-smashed number one in the ear and got to his feet. Number two was lunging for him over the body of number one; Frost swatted him aside in mid-air with the suitbag left by the dresser. Number one was up, his right ready for a haymaker. Frost stepped into it and caught the blow against his left forearm, then crossed the right side of the man's face and mouth with the outer edge of the knife in his right.

Blood sprayed into Frost's face as the killer's left cheek peeled away. He was screaming. Frost didn't have time for another blow. Number two was already on the edge of Frost's peripheral vision. Frost dropped, flexing his knees, then drove into the man's gut, throwing him back across the waterbed. The man had recovered his knife and that was Frost's principal concern.

Frost jammed his left knee down on the man's right wrist, blocking the blade, then laced him across the mouth with a hard left jab. He dove over him, grabbing for the 9mm beside the bed. Number two was tough, he decided. The man came down hard with his knife and Frost felt it slice across the left bicep. The blade ripped through the blankets and into the waterbed. As Frost and the second killer writhed across the bed toward Frost's gun, the rubber smelling water in the mattress of the waterbed suddenly sprayed toward the ceiling like a gusher.

Frost curled the fingers of his right hand around the rubber grips on his pistol as the man stabbed down with the knife again. Frost wrenched sideways as he jacked the hammer back, then pulled the trigger, the first shot catching the man in the throat. The man's hands were still locked onto Frost's shoulders even in death. Number one was still around and Frost looked for him. There was a GI .45 in his fist as he charged the few feet toward the bed.

Number one's first shot thudded into the dead guy's back and bounced him away, off the sagging mattress. Frost got to his feet, stepping away clumsily, his feet on the puddled floor. Frost fired, emptying two rounds, then two more into the first man's center of mass. Rather than knocking him down, the 115-grain JHP's just killed him, the force of his charge hurling his body onto the waterbed, the .45 going off into the mattress and sending up another gusher, the man's body bouncing back and onto the floor.

Frost wheeled toward the door, the High Power in his right fist. No one came through the doorway.

He checked the Rolex on his left wrist. The grazing wound on his left arm from the knife was bothering him, but not much. He almost fell as he crossed the water soaked carpet. There was more of a flood the running shower head had made on the bathroom floor.

Frost pulled on his underpants. Two men not much past twenty stepped through the doorway, wearing blue slacks and blue shirts with badges pinned on them.

One of them shouted, "Freeze!"

Chapter 18

Lots of things were bugging Frost as he looked out on the meager expanse of squat mixed construction buildings and two lane blacktop highway through the seen-better-days venetian blinds across the desk in the police chief's office. The most immediate problem was that he was out of cigarettes. His watch read eight A.M. and he'd been up an even forty-eight hours. He had about another twelve or fourteen hours in him before he'd fall over. His eye still burned with sleeplessness but his head had stopped swimming from it about an hour back. He'd given the Chief Mike O'Hara's twenty-four hour duty number. Mentioning FBI had done the trick.

He had but one idea why the two men had tried to kill him. Eva Chapmann. Frost had followed her to central Florida, then lost her. She apparently hadn't lost him.

The Chief walked in behind Frost then. He could hear the heel cleats on the hard linoleum floor. The man wore the same shirt he'd worn at three-fifteen when he'd raced into the hotel room. It had been white once.

A squat man with bulging muscles, his only badge of authority was a nickel-plated S & W Military & Police with what looked like genuine ivory grips on it in a well-worn holster of ancient design with largely smoothed over flower carving. The holster drooped on his right side from a sagging trouser belt. He sat down across from Frost in a cracking brown leather chair, identical to the one Frost had occupied for the last hour. He said nothing, but trained his best professional "naughty-naughty" blue-eyed glare on Frost. His brow, which extended half-way up to the top of his head, was furrowed and spouting rivulets of sweat so that his face gave the appearance of being freshly basted with melted butter like a Thanksgiving turkey.

"So, Henry Frost is a bit more than an exceptionally unpopular tourist, with equally exceptional self-defense skills. What do your friends call you, Captain Frost?" He leaned back in his chair and fiddled with a pipe. It looked like one of the ones made out of space-age plastic instead of wood. It was green and looked as though it had probably been someone's Christmas present to him.

Frost answered the question. "When I get some friends, I'll let you know." Frost found himself chewing his knuckle for want of a cigarette and stopped it.

"Well, Henry" (that wasn't what anybody ever

95

called Frost and the old man knew it) "your pal would vouch for you but he can't. In the hospital with a coma. Shot-up. But a friend of his—name of Sam Kelsoe—is comin' down over here to pick you up."

"What happened to Mike O'Hara?"

"Kelsoe wouldn't get too specific about it. Said he'd square the thing with those fellas that tried to kill you last night—this morning, I should say. Christ, I'm tired!" He gave up on the pipe and tossed it down on his desk in the basket marked "Out." The Chief turned his chair around a full 360 degrees, looked at Frost again and said, "You're pretty good at killin' people, Henry. Too good."

"There's no such thing as being too good. But I look at it the other way around. I'm pretty good at staying alive. Somebody gets killed trying to keep me from doing that, that's their lookout."

"Nonetheless, a sterling bit of work you did, Henry." He was smiling at Frost and the one-eyed man couldn't read him well that way.

"Actually," Frost grinned, "I'm a little rusty."

"Ah, but it's like swimming or riding a bicycle; may swallow a bit of water or bark your shins every once in a while, but it all comes back to you." He picked up the pipe momentarily, seemingly thought better of it, then said, "Your Mr. Kelsoe said to give you a message. Sit tight and watch your back. Those are his exact words."

"Did Kelsoe say anything to you about getting my guns back?"

"Well, Henry, I asked him about that and he

said that was something he'd work out with me when he got here."

He let a smile come to his lips. "Now, cut out the tough guy routine long enough to go across the street with me to have breakfast. We're both tired, son."

He stood up, gave a hitch to his trousers under the beer pot, another hitch to the gun on his hip and walked toward the door. Frost wasn't hungry by now, just too tired to argue. He got up and followed the Chief, grabbing his jacket. As Frost slipped it on, he was grateful for the shower and change of clothes. Now, just a little sleep . . .

Frost followed the older man through the frosted glass doors reading "Police Department" in big letters and "Edgar Palmer, Chief" in smaller print underneath. They turned down the corridor and went outside. Frost stood on the height of the steps a moment as Chief Palmer buttoned his jacket. It was cold for Florida, frost or a heavy dew still on the grass in the square before them. They marched down the steps of the Police Department cum Fire Department cum City Hall cum Circuit Court and started across the nearly deserted two lane. Frost caught a glimpse of the sun.

A passably good sized restaurant loomed up in front of them: Frost wasn't too sharp that morning—and they went inside. Palmer walked past tables loaded with bleary-eyed truckers and some school kids—it was Saturday, Frost guessed—having nothing better to do than be up so early. They took a booth all the way in the back by the kitchen. Frost told Palmer he'd be back and walked over to the cigarette machine, found some Camels, and had one fired up before he made it back to the booth.

The girl had already brought coffee.

The Chief was taking a stab at another pipe, this time a blue one. Frost could see the scenario clearly. Probably Palmer'd been a heavy smoker. A wife—by the ring on his finger—or maybe his kids had given him a batch of pipes not too long ago and he was trying to use them to quit.

"It doesn't usually help, you know," Frost smiled.

"What's that?" he said.

"Pipes don't usually help you to quit cigarettes. I've tried it a couple times."

He just nodded, still apparently waiting for Frost to say something about the fight in the motel, Frost guessed. He said, "I can't tell you who those guys were—truth."

They stopped talking while the waitress brought more coffee. She poured them each a cup and set the steaming glass pot on the table as she took their orders. After she left, Frost went on. "I'm tracking somebody who tried to kill me. Maybe they worked for her."

"Her?"

"A long story," Frost muttered.

"I thought you didn't have too many friends," he said smiling. "But you must have enemies."

Frost laughed and answered, "Doesn't everybody?"

Palmer finished his second cup of coffee. Frost

noticed the older man's dark blue eyes moving about the crowd, watching the doorway. After the waitress came with their orders—a girl not remarkably pretty but not the opposite either, with a good pair of breasts fighting it out—embarrassedly, Frost guessed—with a shrunken waitress uniform—Palmer asked, "What do you think about the killers or would be killers and their weapons?"

Again, Frost had nothing to hide, so answered him. "They were using professional weapons, elcheapo knives you could buy anywhere. The guns were GI .45s manufactured from parts, probably stolen out of Viet Nam. The gun the one guy tried to get me with was so loose you could shake it and make it rattle. They were wearing surgical rubber gloves so they wouldn't leave prints. If your guys look around the bushes outside or in the restaurant washroom, they'll probably find wallets with some authentic looking phony ID. They'd have kept the ID close by so that they could get to it to look legitimate in a hurry if they had to. There's probably a stolen car with remanufactured plates on it parked in one of the restaurant or motel lots, or maybe a rental car under one of the false names. Nothing that could be traced but something that would look good in a pinch.

"In the old days," Frost went on, suddenly feeling like talking, "they wouldn't have had labels in their clothes, but with mass merchandisers and off the rack stuff, the clothes probably come from a discount store or some other outfit like that, sportscoats and pre-cuffed slacks so no record of alterations would be left. Probably don't have criminal records or prints on file, otherwise they wouldn't have tried for me from up close. But they wore the gloves anyway so that if they got picked up someday, the off-chance of matching their prints from a booking sheet to this wouldn't be something to worry about."

"You make it sound so encouraging, Henry."

"Hank," Frost corrected, "Okay?"

The older man smiled.

Chapter 19

Frost was sitting in Chief Palmer's office again, Palmer having gone out suddenly after a telephone call. Frost watched the street again. It was getting dark outside now. Frost had spent the afternoon sleeping in one of the cells, the door unlocked and the cell ridiculously clean; on a few occasions in Africa and Latin America, and elsewhere, the one-eyed man had become a connoisseur of cells.

Showered, slept and changed, Frost felt almost human. As he started lighting a cigarette, Palmer's door opened. Palmer walked in, then behind him a man with reddish hair, the most wrinkled forehead Frost had ever seen and the look and eyes of a cop.

"Sam Kelsoe, meet Hank Frost—doesn't like it when folks call him Henry," Palmer laughed.

Frost extended his hand, the red-haired man taking it. "Frost, I talked with Chief Palmer; he'll have a lot of paperwork, but everything's set to get you out of here. They'll postpone any inquest until this is settled. I read that telegram you sent to Mike O'Hara; it came after he got shot up. This Eva Chapmann—I think the Bureau wants her more than you do."

"Would somebody tell me what the hell is going on?" Frost asked, starting to feel angry.

"In a little bit. We're gonna get out of the Chief's hair here." Frost smiled at the remark—there wasn't much to get out of. "Then I've got a little checking to do and we can put together the whole number."

"What?"

"Couple things I gotta run down. That name you mentioned in the telegram."

Frost started, "You mean—"

"That's the one," Kelsoe interrupted.

Frost wondered why Kelsoe hadn't wanted him to say Creighton Dean in front of Palmer.

Palmer broke the silence. "Then I guess you're about to get these back."

Frost turned around, looking at the older man. Palmer was unlocking a drawer in his desk, set the keys down on the desk top and beside the keys placed Frost's Metalifed High Power, the spare magazines for it, then the little Gerber MkI Boot Knife, then the KG-9 and the spare magazines for it. "Your luggage and everything is out with my secretary just beyond the door.

"And let me say something, Henry; I enjoyed talkin' to you, but I hope you never come back to my town again."

Frost smiled and extended his hand to the man,

Palmer taking it.

"Good luck, Chief—sorry for the, ahh—"

"The mess—I know. Special Agent Kelsoe there assured me the Bureau would fill me in; I don't believe that but at least it's something to fill up my paperwork with."

As Frost started to follow Kelsoe out the door, feeling slightly stupid holding the KG-9, his Browning in his belt, the magazines and knife in his pockets, Frost decided he didn't believe it either.

Chapter 20

"That Creighton Dean guy is Senator Creighton Dean—ex-Senator anyway," Sam Kelsoe said, sitting down opposite Frost at the corner booth near the telephone he'd just left. His red eyebrows were knit tight together in his furrowed forehead.

"A Senator?" Frost repeated.

"Yeah—a Senator. Big in missile and aircraft guidance systems; manufactured a lot of the hardware for the space shuttle program."

"The space shuttle," Frost repeated, looking up as the waitress brought him more coffee. The juke box was playing, a country western song Frost couldn't quite identify.

Across the street, Frost could see the lights in Chief Palmer's office, still burning.

Frost shifted the weight of the Browning in the Alessi Rig under his jacket, then looked across the table at Kelsoe. "The space shuttle? What the hell would Eva Chapmann have to do with the space shuttle and some ex-Senator? That's—"

"Yeah, well, whatever—but there's a launch in two days and if some broad like Eva Chapmann—what was it you said the natives called her?"

"The Deathwitch," Frost said quietly, lighting a Camel.

"Yeah—well, if this Deathwitch has something to do with Creighton Dean that might mean something going on against the space shuttle; you said she had it in for the United States, right? That's a prestige thing—the shuttle program."

"What happened to Mike O'Hara?" Frost interrupted.

"Got a tip through our regular drug contacts in Columbia that a plane was leaving for Central Florida; that's nothin' new."

"But that's DEA—not FBI."

"Yeah—but the Colombian authorities didn't think it had drugs—crates of assault rifles and other stuff. So DEA contacted Customs and it eventually wound up with us and that anti-terrorist detail Mike is on, most of the time. Well, Mike and a dozen of our guys went down there—about sixty miles from here, couple counties over. There was a whole reception committee waiting for the plane. Some blonde-haired woman and about eighteen guys. Big shoot-out. The plane got airborne, the arms—spotted a lot of stuff before they closed in—got unloaded, picked up. Just when Mike led the bust, well—shooting started. All our guys had was mostly handguns,

105

few assault rifles and riot shotguns. They had sub-machineguns—one of them had a belt-fed machinegun going. Mike and a bunch of guys bought it—five of our guys got killed, two cops from the State Police, a customs agent got wounded. Mike's in a coma; don't know if he'll ever get out of it. Used to tell me all about you; how crazy you are—"

"Hell," Frost smiled, staring into his coffee. "O'Hara's the crazy one. I'm normal compared to him."

"But he always talked like you were a good guy—you know? Well—I talked it over with my supervisor, and he talked it over with the Deputy Director—seems they know you too, from that deal with the plot to assassinate the President.* Both you guys got shot up, I remember."

"Yeah," Frost murmured, still looking at his coffee.

"Well—the Deputy Director okayed the deal—if you wanna get in on it. And there isn't much choice, is there?"

"What deal?"

"Looks like this Chapmann dame and the dame with the arms shipment are one and the same."

"Bank on it," Frost said, looking up, studying Kelsoe's face.

"We do. Well, when I got the word on Dean when I was on the phone there," and Kelsoe pointed behind Frost, who only nodded. "Hell—

*See, They Call Me The Mercenary #8, Assassin's Express

Dean's too big for us to run up to him and say, 'Hey—you doin' somethin' with this mercenary broad they gave the name of Deathwitch to?' We can't. Not yet. But we worked somethin' out.''

"What?'' Frost asked.

"Well, Dean's got a daughter—lives back east—Back Bay type, right? Well, I know a way of gettin' you an introduction to her. Real classy dame, I guess. We'll fix you up with money, loan you a car—the whole shot. You get a little tight with her—''

"Hey—wait a minute. I'm a mercenary sometimes, sometimes I'm in executive protection—I'm no lounge lizard spy.''

"Yeah. Well, you use your right name. If she's into something with her father, or even if she isn't in on it and just her father is, well—once your name gets to him, Eva Chapmann's bound to come after you. Once we flush this Deathwitch dame out into the open, we can close in on her. And that'd give us the tip into Dean himself. Piece of cake.''

"I can see why O'Hara's crazy—hangs around with you.''

"Will ya do it?''

Frost thought back to the fight in his hotel room. "Yeah—can't keep a gun in the shower with me very well, can I? When do we leave?''

Kelsoe was already getting up, starting back to the phone. "I got a helicopter standing by to get us to the airport in Miami—how's ten minutes grab ya?''

Frost looked up at Kelsoe; he didn't find it amusing at all.

Chapter 21

It had to be just right so it wouldn't be obvious. Kelsoe had briefed Frost on Sandra Dean, set him up with a fast tailoring job on four three-piece suits and a tuxedo and the stuff to go with it and arranged for him to have two cars. One, a current model Lincoln Continental, he was about to wreck, on purpose. Frost smiled at the thought. The other, a Datsun 280ZX, had a little special something Kelsoe had left in the trunk in case Eva Chapmann's men closed in too fast. Eva Chapmann's and Creighton Dean's men, Frost mentally corrected himself.

The thing looked vaguely like a vintage Thompson submachinegun, but with a space age twist. Instead of .45 ACP slugs, though, it fired 40mm grenades. Frost couldn't see himself needing it, but hadn't argued when Kelsoe had run the controls of the thing by him.

During the flight from Miami to Boston, Kelsoe had briefed Frost on Creighton Dean's illustrious career: Senator, political leader, industrialist, minor league genius. And very acquisitive, whether a corporate merger, political power or whatever, Dean had a track record of always wanting to have it, or doing anything to get it.

Sandra Dean—Frost ran the details by himself as he waited, the rain pouring down, the parking lot deserted of people and crammed with cars. She was blonde-haired, twenty-six years old and collected men like some women collected doll furniture.

Frost hadn't seen himself as that collectible, but Kelsoe had insisted Frost give it a try. Without meeting the woman, Frost had already decided he didn't like her.

He saw her then, running across the parking lot on high heels, a plastic see-through umbrella over her head, a mink coat wrapped around her. She stopped beside a Bentley, apparently hadn't locked it, pulled open the door (slamming into a Volkswagen parked beside the Bentley) and disappeared inside.

Frost turned the ignition switch on the Lincoln, flicking on his own windshield wipers as he watched the wiper blades on the Bentley start to move. Frost released the emergency brake and put the transmission into drive.

The Bentley was already moving as Frost pulled out of his parking spot.

Kelsoe had said Sandra Dean would make a left out of the lot—to her hairdresser's. Frost hoped the heavy rain hadn't caused the woman to cancel her appointment.

Frost would make a right, just so she could pile into him.

Frost reached the edge of the driveway, waiting at the sidewalk. An old man and a little girl were walking slowly past him, under an umbrella. Frost watched the exit drive to his right. Sandra Dean was ready to make her turn, the parking attendant's hut separating the two drives.

The old man and little girl were nearly past. Frost glanced to his right, seeing the Bentley edging forward. "Shit!"

The old man and little girl were past and Frost stepped on the gas, making a sharp right into the largely deserted street.

His body shook with the impact as he slammed on the brakes. The one-eyed man looked out through the right side passenger window.

The Bentley had broadsided him and was stopped.

The girl wasn't getting out. He could see her face a little through the rain streaked windows.

Frost climbed out from behind the wheel, the transmission in park.

He walked around behind his car, seeing the old man and little girl watching. He smiled at the little girl.

Frost walked up to the driver's side of the Bentley. The window was all the way up.

Rain was dripping down Frost's face and despite the fact he'd engineered the accident, the woman's seemingly uncaring attitude was making him angry. Frost hammered his right fist on the driver's side window. He could see her through it, turning to look at him. The window rolled down automatically a few inches.

"Look what you did to my car, lady," Frost shouted through the rain.

"I'll pay for its repair," she smiled.

"Ohhh," Frost said, trying to let the steam out of his disposition.

"I've never been introduced to a man with an eyepatch before." She was looking at Frost strangely.

"You haven't yet, lady," Frost snarled. He mentally shrugged, remembering he was trying to meet her, not alienate her.

"What's your name?"

"Hank Frost," the one-eyed man told her, his tone softening as he watched the muscles around her eyes tense briefly. "What's yours?"

"Sandra Dean. We don't need the police for this, Mr. Frost, do we? I could write you a check now that would cover the damages, or perhaps we might get together this evening and by then you might have the exact figure."

"I had something else I was going to—"

"That's a shame—"

"I could break it," Frost told her.

"That's good. I'll give you my card—here," and she fished through her purse. Frost thought he caught sight of a metallic object, but it didn't seem to be a gun. "Eight-thirty? I know a wonderful place in one of the suburban areas not far from my house—there's a little map on the back of the card. Shows just how to find my place."

Frost couldn't pass it up. "I don't kiss on the first date."

"I do—ohh, that little place? Black tie if you can."

Frost looked at her and smiled. "If all I wear is a black tie, I'll catch cold."

"You're very amusing. Eight-thirty?"

"Eight-thirty, give or take a few minutes."

"Fine, Mr. Frost." The window rolled up and Frost stepped back as the Bentley started backing up.

She cut the wheels sharp right, swerved past his car, then sharp left as she evened out, the Bentley moving fast down the street away from him.

Frost looked behind him, saw the little girl and the old man, the little girl staring at him.

Frost smiled at the little girl, gesturing down the street after the Bentley. "We just bumped into each other. That was a joke—hmmm?" The little girl didn't laugh. Frost shrugged his soaked through shoulders and stared down at his wrecked car, happy it was borrowed from the federal government.

Chapter 22

The pretty, blonde-haired girl said, "Are you ready, darling?"

Frost, feeling stupid in a tuxedo, answered, "That's my line, isn't it Sandra?"

She smiled and said, "I suppose I said it because I was ready." Frost smiled and as he took a last sip at his drink, put money down on the bar. The bartender gave him a knowing wink.

Frost helped her slip into her mink coat, then turned to the barman and shrugged. Frost and the girl walked out into the night, steam rising on their breath. The doorman whistled and after a moment Frost's car was brought around. As the doorman helped the girl into the car, he knocked her handbag to the ground and, as he picked it up, spilled it open. Apologizing, he said, "I'm sorry to be so clumsy, Miss."

Frost said, "No harm done, I suppose," and watched as the doorman replaced the articles—one of them a pager device.

As Frost got in the driver's seat, he handed the doorman a tip and the man said, "Thank you, sir."

Frost added an extra five to the tip, saying, "Thank you."

After driving the borrowed 280ZX through the city streets, Frost turned onto a side road, quickly heading up a narrow rocky road along the seacoast winding toward a high promontory. Some twenty miles later he stopped the sportscar in the circular driveway of a well-appointed two-story house at the height of the promontory. Helping the girl out of the car, Frost followed her up a winding flight of stone steps to the outside door, then taking her proffered key, let them in.

Once inside the door, Frost reached under his jacket. She flicked on the lights. Frost gently eased his hand out from his jacket and with the other hand retrieved his battered Zippo lighter. "Ah, there it is."

As he started to take a cigarette, the girl touched his hand and said, "Wait, Hank, I'll offer you something you'll like better."

Frost took her in his arms, their lips almost touching, saying to her, "And what would that be?"

She smiled and took his hand and he followed her up the steps to her bedroom. Once inside the door, she turned toward him and wrapped her arms around his neck, kissing him. She pushed away from him and fell back across the bed, Frost beside her. As he kissed her, she wriggled free,

115

breathless, saying, "Wait a moment, darling. I'll be right back," and, barefoot, she ran toward the bathroom.

Frost rolled over on his side, his eye surveying the bedroom, coming to rest on a huge woodburning fireplace. Absently, the fire burning there bothered him. Seeing her by the bathroom door again, a towel wrapped around her, she started to reach for the toggle-style light switch. As she did, Frost rolled off the bed, the electric current arced across it, the bedspread smoldering.

"Electric blanket gone bad?" Frost quipped, his right hand sliding under his jacket.

"But how could you . . ."

Frost cut her off mid-sentence: "Easy kid—you were too easy. And besides all the rest of the light switches in the house seem to be rheostat models. That one you just pressed was a regular switch. And you were making such a damn production out of the whole thing."

She screamed, shouting, "You one-eyed bast—" The word died in the sound of the bedroom door crashing open, men streaming through as Frost wheeled. His Metalifed Browning in his fist, Frost grappled with the first man through the door, knocking him aside with a backhanded smash to the teeth with the pistol butt, then kicking him in the rear end at the base of the spine, sending him hurtling onto the bed, the electric shock arcing through the man's body as he screamed. As the second man came at him, Frost sidestepped, wheeling, lashing out with his left foot in a high kick to the man's chin, knocking him back through the open doorway. A third man was coming, tackling Frost and bringing him down. Frost's Browning clattered to the floor, sliding across the room. He smashed the knuckles of both fists into the man's rib cage, then the base of his hand into the distended jaw. On his feet, Frost's knee smashed the third man in the face.

A fourth man, taller, thin, came at him. Frost snatched the butt end of a burning log from the fireplace, swinging it baseball bat style, setting the fourth attacker on fire as Frost struck him in the face. The man crashed blindly through the bedroom window, screaming, falling to the rocks below. Frost wheeled, a fifth man rushing him, almost shoving Frost through the broken window. Frost elbowed the man in the side of the head, wheeled and smashed with his other elbow to the same side, then drove his left to the solar plexus and smashed the man backhanded on the carotid artery. The fifth man dropped.

Getting his balance, Frost started for the doorway. The girl, Sandra, was there, holding his pistol. Frost started to turn away, then kicked out with his right foot, knocking the Browning away, then sidestepped in back of her, kicking her in the rear end, knocking her onto the dead man on the bed. She shrieked as the voltage hit her. Picking up his gun, Frost snarled. "Keep cookin'."

The one-eyed man started through the doorway. At the head of the stairs, he fired twice, downing an armed man rushing toward him. Frost vaulted the railing to the living room floor.

117

Coming through the door from the outside were two more men. Frost fired wildly at them, tossing a sparking and burning lamp, the cord ripped, through the picture window. He snatched up a seat cushion to protect his face, then dove through the window in a shower of glass.

On his feet again, he vaulted the steps to the driveway, reaching his car.

Men were firing at him through the broken window. Gunning the motor, Frost threw the car into gear, roaring down the narrow driveway.

As he turned down the mountain road, two cars and a black van started after him, waiting there to cut him off, Frost guessed. The lead car was coming up fast, men with submachineguns leaning from each side, firing at him.

Frost cut his wheel hard right, then hard left, downshifting to build up RPMs, then upshifting fast, double clutching, third, then fourth gear. Someone in one of the vehicles behind him was firing a riot shotgun—Frost didn't have time to look and see who.

He rounded the Datsun past a bend in the road, starting to downshift—two cars were racing toward him, a submachinegun firing from the window of the car on his left.

Frost cut his wheel hard, the Datsun bouncing off the pavement and streaking onto the sandy incline leading down toward the sea.

He downshifted into first, giving the car all the gas he could as it pitched and skidded, hunting traction in the sand and gravel.

A massive flat rock, low to the ground, loomed ahead of him. The one-eyed man tried cutting the wheel, but the steering wouldn't respond quickly enough, the low slung sports car impacting against the rock, bouncing up and stalling out on it. As the car shuddered, Frost felt like every bone in his body was able to feel it.

The cars and the van were coming, five vehicles in all, the van leading as it streaked down toward the beach.

Frost piled out of the car, pulling open his bow tie as he did, popping the button on his shirt collar. "Damn tuxedo," he snarled.

He fumbled the key into the trunk, popping the trunk lid, reaching inside.

Kelsoe had put it there, given Frost the operating instructions when he'd given Frost the car. Kelsoe had warned Frost that the men he'd be up against played rough.

Frost ducked beside the Datsun, the van coming, submachineguns blazing from the open windows. "I can play rough too," he said to himself. He rotated the safety off safe to the firing mode, the Hawk Engineering MM-1 in his hands like a Thompson submachinegun. His left fist was knotted around the front grip, his right on the rear grip, his first finger against the revolver style trigger. The chamber housing was already wound, loaded with twelve #406 40mm High Explosive projectiles.

As the one-eyed man lined up the MM-1, he ran the stats by in his mind. Twelve rounds, fired semi-automatic. Penetrates two inches of armor plate—he guessed that covered vans and passenger cars okay. Fifteen meter kill radius.

The van was closing now. Frost squeezed the trigger, the MM-1 bucking in his hands no more than a twelve gauge. He could hear the whistling sound of the 40mm projectile, it impacting against the van, the van seeming to blow upward, outward, and inward all at the same time, a massive fireball searing skyward into the night.

The noise of the explosion was almost deafening, and sand was raining down on Frost now as he crouched nearer the car. As the fire cleared, Frost could see the chunks of wreckage, the black crater in the sand and gravel. The van had all but disintegrated.

Frost smiled. "Gotta get me one of these," he laughed getting up to his feet, taking a step forward, aiming the MM-1 at the nearest of the four automobiles. There was a subgunner leaning out of the front passenger seat, his bullets impacting on the sand a dozen yards ahead of Frost. Frost fired the MM-1, then fired it again. He could only hear one of the whistling sounds. The first projectile impacted into the sand in front of the car, the second hitting the car itself. Sand showered down, almost burying the car as the car itself exploded.

Frost turned the muzzle of the MM-1, firing again, at the next car, the car rocking skyward, exploding in mid-air.

Frost fired again, then once more, knocking out the third car; it rolled down the embankment, burning, pieces of metal flying from it.

The fourth car was already stopped, men running from it, not shooting, scrambling up the embankment for their lives.

Frost fired, one projectile blowing the car.

He swung the muzzle of the MM-1, then fired toward the men. He only got the nearer man, the body vanishing in a puff of fire.

"Needs more elevation," he murmured, raising the muzzle and firing. Once, then once again. The hillside was for an instant an inferno, the fleeing gunmen lost in it.

Frost looked at the MM-1, nodded to himself and set it back in the open trunk.

The 280ZX's tires were lost in the sand and gravel, and getting the car out would be hopeless without a tow truck. The one-eyed man shrugged, slammed the trunk shut, then started to walk diagonally across the embankment, up toward the road. He imagined with all the noise, someone—like the police—would be coming along soon enough. He tossed the car keys into the sand so the police couldn't make him open the trunk. He didn't feel like waiting it out for Sam Kelsoe in a jail cell.

Chapter 23

"Do I have to give the suits back?" Frost asked, looking across at Kelsoe, sitting beside him in the back seat of the Ford LTD.

"No—you're wearing one now, aren't you?"

"All in the line of duty," Frost smiled.

"Here—just in case Senator Dean asks to see them—the credentials saying you're in CIA. God—this is stupid," Kelsoe snarled, biting the first knuckle of his left forefinger.

Frost lit a cigarette. "Look, we agreed that if Sandra Dean tried setting me up, then we had something on her father."

"But that's your word against his. We put her in the hospital under a fake name, got her buttoned up tighter than a drum, so she can't tell him what went on. As far as he probably knows, she's dead or in hiding. We're keeping her out for the count as long as we can; but just remember, Dean still has political connections that could rip us apart. There was no official story, so if he knows who you are, you know she set you up through him. That was midnight last night—I make the blackout good for another couple of hours."

"That's why I've gotta see Dean now—catch him a little off balance. The last person he's going to expect calling on him from CIA is me because his daughter and those guys were supposed to kill me. Because if he works with Eva Chapmann, he knows all about me, engineered the set-up last night. And as long as he's in the dark about his daughter, he can't go overtly after me. Maybe we can find out something."

"Or maybe you can get yourself killed," Kelsoe added.

"If Dean tries killing me in his own office, he's crazy. I don't think he's crazy. The space shuttle takes off tomorrow morning. We don't have time to pussy-foot around if Dean and Eva Chapmann are planning something. Neither do they. I'm just going to walk in there and figure out what to say as I go; play it by ear, or maybe by eye," and Frost tugged at his eyepatch.

"What are you gonna say?"

Frost looked at Kelsoe, stubbing out his cigarette then, "Dean owned that property where O'Hara and those guys got into the shoot-out with Eva Chapmann's men. I'll walk in on Dean about that. He's already had the police, the FBI, everybody else up there. May as well have me. Logical thing for him to do is either put me off or offer to help. Either way, he'll be setting me up."

"But if we follow you—"

"You can't; that'd blow the set-up before he tries. But once he tries, if he doesn't get me, then he'll have to go to ground, come out in the open. Then maybe—"

"Hey," Kelsoe exclaimed looking at Frost. "Why are you doing all this?"

"Eva Chapmann left me going blind in the jungle. Her people put O'Hara in the hospital, in a coma—maybe he won't come out of it. As long as Eva Chapmann's alive, well—O'Hara ever mention Bess Stallman?"

"Your girl—yeah. Said she—"

"I know—too good for me," Frost laughed. "Well, he's right. But anyway, as long as Eva Chapmann's out there, alive, Bess and I will never have a moment where we can walk down a street without turning around to look behind us. I don't have much choice, do I?"

The car stopped, Frost looking out the window. A massive office building dominated his view. A sign on the manicured lawn read, "Dean International—Guidance Systems Division."

"Frost—I hate leavin' you here."

"I'll call you if I need a ride—maybe I can bum a ride back from Dean."

Frost stepped out of the car, tugging his vest down, reaching back inside for the borrowed attaché case—three adventure novels, a banana and a pad of yellow paper and a Bic pen were inside. "See ya," the one-eyed man smiled. But as he turned toward the Dean Building, his smile faded.

Frost walked toward the large glass doors with DEAN in gold letters across them. Getting directions from the starter, he entered an elevator and the starter turned the key. Only one floor was listed—"Penthouse." As the elevator doors opened, Frost stepped out into a carpeted reception area. A beautiful, dark-haired woman was sitting at a receptionist's desk. She smiled and asked, "May I help you?"

"Yes," Frost answered, smiling, resting his attaché case on the edge of her desk, "My name is Hank Frost—C.I.A. I have an appointment with Senator Dean."

"Yes, he's expecting you, Mister Frost. Would you follow me please?"

"Sure," Frost grunted, catching up his attaché case and walking after her through carved oak double doors. The inner office was a huge oval. Curved tinted glass picture windows looked out over greater Miami and the ocean. A huge antique desk with a leather swivel chair commanded the office, the office carpeted like the outer office in maroon pile. Leather couches and chairs studded the room and a black leather padded bar was off in the corner, diagonally opposite the desk. The girl gestured Frost toward the large leather easy chair directly opposite the desk. The dark-haired receptionist asked, "Would you care for some coffee or tea, Mister Frost?"

Frost replied, "Thank you, but no."

"Senator Dean will be with you shortly, Mister Frost." The girl retired from the room. Frost's eye swept the room and came to rest on a light fixture. He guessed it concealed a television camera. He smiled in the direction of the fixture and waved.

Frost turned when he heard the voice behind him. "How clever of you to notice the camera, Mister Frost. But then such a device must appear so unsophisticated to someone such as yourself."

Frost shrugged, getting up and shaking Dean's outstretched right hand. "Please, Mister Frost, sit down. Somehow I feel we know each other."

Frost, forcing a smile, said, "Somehow, I feel the same way."

Dean, lighting a small cigar and offering one to Frost, who refused it with a nod, said, "But then, Mister Frost, I'm sure you didn't come to discuss that."

"Actually," Frost began, "I'd hoped you might be in a position to shed some light on the shoot-out on your ranch property—that is to say some details you might have neglected to mention to the FBI or the police."

"I can't think of anything, Mister Frost."

Flourishing his cigar, Dean went on, "Something tells me terrorists. I don't know," Dean added, "I've personally directed my security force to use all the resources of Dean International if necessary to assist in the investigation. You see, since it was my property and all that where the incident took place, I feel personally responsible."

"I can understand that better than you might realize, Senator."

Dean asked, "Perhaps you might like to meet my security chief and view some of our training effort. I'll confess, firearms and violence leave me quite mystified. But I'm sure you'd find our training facility quite interesting. It's located below ground level. Shall we?" Dean said, rising.

As Frost started to pick up his attaché case, Dean said, "You can leave that here if you like, Mister Frost."

Frost, smiling and picking up the case, said, "That's most kind, but I might want to take notes. Anyway—my banana's inside. Might get hungry."

"Quite," said Dean, smiling, leading the way to another private elevator. There was a door leading from inside his office and through a corridor, paralleling the main elevator banks, Frost guessed. Dean used a key and they entered.

Frost and Dean rode in silence to the sub-basement of the building. As the doors opened, muted gunfire and the grunting sounds of men in martial arts training filled the air. Dean, lighting a fresh cigar from a small leather case, talked as Frost walked alongside him. "This is the nerve center of my security force, Mister Frost. As I'm sure you are aware, an international firm such as mine must be nearly as concerned with intelligence and security matters as a nation these days. I'm only sorry some of my men weren't around during that battle with the arms smugglers. The outcome might have been different."

"No disrespect intended to your force, but I

rather doubt that, Senator," Frost smiled.

As they continued walking, they passed a massive—and expensive—indoor range with riot shotgun practice in progress.

Frost's ears rang as he noticed a tall, dark-haired, good looking man in black slacks and black turtleneck. The man was coming toward them.

"Senator Dean."

"Piersen, I'd like you to meet Mister Frost—he tells us he's with C.I.A." Piersen and Frost shook hands as Dean said, "Mister Frost, this is my security chief and personal bodyguard, Phillip Piersen. As you might doubtless ask, where was he the evening of the gunfight? Unfortunately, a pressing family matter called him away."

Frost, smiling, said, "I hope it wasn't a death, Mister Piersen."

Piersen, grinning, said, "Not yet, Mister Frost. But any time now." Then, putting his hand on Frost's shoulder, he added, "I noticed your interest in that range. Care to have a look?"

"Seen one riot gun, you've seen 'em all," the one-eyed man answered.

Piersen joined them as they walked, saying to Frost, "We strive for a level of training here superior to that of the best secret service and counter-terrorist organizations in the world, such as the Israeli Mossad, the West German—"

"The C.I.A.?" Frost interrupted.

"Yes, exactly," Piersen continued. "And, we can afford better and more up-to-date equipment.

Only the latest and the best."

"Really."

"Yes," Piersen smiled. "But you should enjoy this, Mister Frost." Strolling round the corner to a glass enclosed arena, Piersen said, "We have our own system of martial arts training, combining the best of Kung Fu, Karate, Judo, Aikido and the other oriental arts, plus the French Savate."

Frost paused to glance into the glass enclosed area below them. A tall, beautiful, athletic looking girl in a karate suit, shoulder length hair floating out around her as she maneuvered, was fighting a man twice her size. "Who's that, the young woman?" Frost asked.

Dean interposed. "That's our Felicity Grey. Piersen tells me she's one of our best agents. She's fighting Chup Teng, our chief martial arts instructor. Care for a closer look?"

"Yes, if you don't mind," Frost answered.

As they walked down the steps into the arena, Dean quipped to Piersen, "It appears we've finally found something to catch Mister Frost's eye. This way."

Immediately, as they stepped into the arena, the massive, bald Chup Teng clapped his hands and the bout stopped. Piersen stepped forward to introduce them. "Mister Frost, this is Chup Teng, perhaps the most formidable adversary in hand-to-hand combat in the world, possessor of black belts in all the disciplines and the highest honors in world competitions. And this is Miss Grey."

129

Frost took the girl's hand in his and their eyes met. With her other hand, she brushed back a strand of hair and then smiled, "I'm happy to meet you, Mister Fost."

As Frost made to speak, Piersen interrupted, saying, "I'm sure you're quite talented in hand-to-hand combat yourself, Mister Frost. Care for a round with Chup Teng?"

Frost looked at Piersen, saying nothing. Dean, in an affable tone, puffing on a fresh cigar, said, "Piersen, you're embarrassing Mister Frost. After all, no one is a match for Chup Teng."

"Go ahead, Mister Frost," Piersen said, "as a personal favor. But—maybe Senator Dean is right. It was rude of me to suggest it. You couldn't hope to fight Chup Teng and win."

Frost glanced at the girl, then set down his attaché case. Chup Teng began to laugh. The huge Oriental walked to the corner of the arena where several bricks for striking practice were stacked. He smashed them to dust with the heel of his bare foot. Using his index finger, he thrust into a punching bag and burst it, then laughed again. Taking a Miami phone book from an equipment table, he ripped it in half; then, laughing, bit through one of the halves, discarding the phone book. Frost continued to step out of his sixty-five dollar shoes.

"Really, Mister Frost," Dean said. "I wouldn't know what to do if you were to be injured."

"I'm sure you'd think of something," Frost nodded.

Dean, smiling, said, "May I hold your coat, at least?"

Frost, half-turning away from Chup Teng to answer, said, "Thanks, but it really won't take me that long. Watch my banana." As he said the last word, and Dean chuckled through a cloud of cigar smoke, Frost, still turned half-away from the huge Oriental, lashed out with his right foot, catching the man in the adam's apple. As the Oriental's hand went up to it, automatically, Frost struck again with his foot, this time to the solar plexus. As the Oriental began to double over, Frost backhanded him with his right fist, then wheeled into the Oriental with his left elbow, then his right, striking at the head and face and throat, then smashed with the arch of his foot to the groin. Frost crossed his left knee into the side of the Oriental's head. He drew back his right for a blow with the heel of the hand to the Oriental's face, but as the huge man rocked in semi-consciousness, Frost turned his back and lightly pushed the Oriental on the chest with his left hand and the man collapsed in a heap. "There, Senator," Frost said, straightening his tie and brushing back the hair from his forehead, "I told you it wouldn't take very long. How's my banana?"

Frost eyed Piersen as the man started reaching behind his back and under his sweater. Dean stepped between them. "Yes, you did, didn't you, Mister Frost. Is there anything else we can show you?"

131

"No," Frost answered.

The girl, her eyes looking at him approvingly, smiled.

"I was going to suggest something of which I'm sure you'll approve, Mister Frost. Miss Grey joined our organization less than a year ago, but already she's done admirable service." Frost looked hard at Dean as he went on. "If you would allow me, I'd like to place Miss Grey under you—to take you to the scene of the shoot-out on my ranch."

"What a nice idea," Frost smiled.

"Perhaps," Dean continued, "Perhaps—though I'm certainly not knowledgeable in things such as this—it might help. A fresh insight might yield some clue to the terrorists' identities which the police and FBI overlooked. With Miss Grey to accompany you, I'm sure it would be well worth it."

"You think so, Senator?" Frost said, stepping back into his sixty-five dollar shoes.

"Oh, I do indeed," Dean said. "You'll get into something, I'm sure, with Miss Grey's help. Get the lay of the land, as they say, at the very least."

"I'll change, sir, I won't be a moment," the girl said, and ran off, turning her face away.

As they followed her up the steps, Dean turned to Frost and said, "Before you leave, Mister Frost, you must tell us what you thought of our training center." Dean clapped Frost on the shoulder, biting down on his cigar.

Frost turned to him and smiled, "Since you

asked, I definitely feel the martial arts program is somewhat wanting," and turned to glance back at the Oriental, stirring on the floor, some of Dean's men trying to help him up.

Chapter 24

A ribbon of two-lane highway running parallel to the sea opened beyond a curve, over the hood of the Fiat Turbo, the top down. The girl, her hair caught up in the wind, was driving. She said, "Beautiful day, isn't it, Mister Frost?"

"Call me Hank."

"All right, Hank. My first name is Felicity."

"That's a strange name, but a pretty one."

She turned and looked at him, then smiled before looking back to the road.

Frost asked, "Tell me, Felicity; what got you working for Senator Dean?"

"Senator Dean promised me a very rewarding job."

"I'm sure," Frost said, turning to look away into the passenger side racing mirror.

The girl's voice made him turn to face her as she spoke. "I'm damned fed up with all the double entendres. I went to work for Senator

Dean for a good salary and good fringe benefits—and before that causes a raised eyebrow, I mean hospital benefits and profit sharing!"

"I'm sorry," Frost said, reaching out to touch her hand. She went to draw it away, but didn't. "Senator Dean brings out the worst in me, I'm afraid."

"I know," she answered. "He talks one way, acts another."

"You seem too professional for an industrial security team. You're good with Karate—you mentioned you have a pilot's license. But then you know that." Frost glanced into the mirror again.

"I guess that's a compliment," she said. "Thank you."

"Senator Dean must be one of the richest men in the world," Frost remarked.

"I guess he always wants more and it doesn't matter how he gets it—not at all. Just the winning counts."

"Senator Dean is very much involved in the electronic guidance apparatus used in the space shuttle program, isn't he?" Frost remarked.

"Yes, tracking and guidance systems; that sort of thing," Felicity answered. "He's a very successful man." Pausing a moment, she went on, "Will the space shuttle be delayed now. Have you heard of the auxiliary power unit problem they've been having?"

"No," Frost said, turning in his seat to look behind them. "The space shuttle won't be delayed—I don't think—but we might."

"What do you mean?" she asked, alarmed.

"Look into your mirror." Behind Frost and the girl were three vans. "Do you recognize those?"

"No, should I?"

"Maybe. They might belong to your illustrious employer, Senator Dean."

The girl shot a glance over her shoulder, then half-shouted, "All right. Here we go!" On the last word, she double clutched and down shifted to rev the engine and then upshifted onto the straightaway. The black vans upped their speed as well as Frost looked back, the oversized tires screeching on the asphalt.

Frost holding onto the sides of his seat, the girl downshifted for a curve, skidded into the hairpin, then stomped down on the gas pedal, twisting the wheel straight as the car accelerated. Frost shouted to her over the roar of the wind, "You almost spun out!"

"No, I didn't, dammit," she screamed, throwing a glance at him. "Just because I'm a woman, do you think I can't drive? That was a modified flick turn!"

"I'll say one thing. It damn well modified my heart rate!" Frost shouted.

The girl, wrestling through another curve, shouted, "What?"

Frost, still holding on, his knuckles white, rasped, "Nothing, kid, just keep your eyes on the road."

The girl glared back at him as she pulled out of another curve, then snorted, "Hmmph!"

The Fiat Turbo skidded into another curve, then fishtailed out along a straightaway. Frost shouted, "Try to hold her steady; I'm going to try to hit that lead van!"

Frost was already reaching under his jacket as he twisted around to kneel in the front passenger seat. Stretching his upper body out across the rear end of the girl's car, Frost levelled the Browning in both hands, tried steadying it, then fired a two-round burst.

The one-eyed man could see his bullets ricochet off the road just in front of the lead van. The van swerved a moment, but kept on coming.

Frost slid down into his seat, shouting over the slipstream, "When we get around that bend in the road, slow down. We're changing seats!"

"No, we're not!" she screamed, glaring at him.

As they rounded the bend, Frost reached over in front of her and turned off the key, then grabbed onto the wheel to control the car, reaching around behind her. "Sorry, kid," Frost pushed her over his lap and slipped into the seat behind the wheel. Restarting the car with the clutch, he downshifted into second to build up RPMs and accelerated through third and fourth, weaving across the highway. Bullets from the submachinegunners firing from the two vans pinged against the little Fiat's body work.

Frost downshifted into third, going into a curve. A huge black and gold painted eighteen-wheeler was blocking all four lanes. The girl was shouting, "My God! You're not going to try driv-

137

ing under that are you?''

Frost, shooting a glance toward her as he wrenched back on the transmission and cut the wheel hard left, shouted back, "Of course not! You can only do that in the movies!"

Frost completed the flick turn, heading the Fiat Turbo back toward the black vans, two of them lined up across the highway, subgunners locking onto the sportscar. The subgunners opened fire as Frost wove the Fiat between them, clipping both his front fenders on the sides of the vans. One of the subgunners had kept firing, not dodging out of the way, and a burst raked the van behind Frost, on his right. In the rearview mirror, the one-eyed man could see it burst into flame.

Frost cut off on a side road leading off the main highway, the road dissipating into a rutted sand and gravel construction road. The two remaining vans, subgunners firing into the road on both sides of the Fiat, were close behind. At the end of the construction road, Frost could see a bridge. He started accelerating.

Frost downshifted the Fiat, bursting the nose of the tiny car through the wooden construction barrier, eyeing the signs reading, "Bridge Out Ahead," as he streaked past them.

Frost slammed on the brakes, downshifting to use engine compression, the car going into a skid, one of the front tires slipping over the edge of the partially disassembled bridge. Working frantically through the gear box, Frost got the Fiat into reverse, the tires screeching as he flick-turned,

138

then started back down the bridge. Lined up at the entrance to the bridge were the two black vans. Subgunners firing from the windows were chewing the flooring of the old wooden bridge to shreds under the Fiat as Frost sped toward them.

Frost shouted to the girl, "All right—hold on!" then cut the wheel hard to the right, the Fiat Turbo punching through the guardrailing and over the side of the bridge, bouncing down onto the dirt embankment at the side of the construction pit below. The rear wheels were churning mounds of dirt. The girl screamed as the passenger side door fell off. The muffler ripped away—Frost could see it in the dirt behind the car. He slipped and skidded into the construction pit and started to cross it.

The ground was flat and even, like a road now. Frost accelerated out of a curve. Then the one-eyed man stomped on the brakes. On both sides and to the front were concrete walls going straight up some twenty feet. A ladder leaned down the wall immediately in front of the car.

The engine still running, Frost shouted, "Time to stretch our legs!" He grabbed the girl by the hand. Pulling her after him, he ran toward the ladder; he pushed her up ahead of him. Already losing a sandal running from the car, the girl kicked off the other shoe and started up the rungs.

Frost was hanging from the ladder two thirds of the way up now, firing the Metalifed Browning. One of the vans had gotten down into the construction pit and two subgunners were climbing out of it. The Browning empty, he stuffed it into his belt and kept climbing.

Frost looked down, two men armed with SMGs, coming up the ladder. Frost leaned over the side of the concrete wall, throwing his weight against the ladder. The ladder toppled back, the subgunners dropping from it, into the dirt.

At the height of the culvert where Frost and the girl stood stretched an open field. Overhead, Frost heard a plane. He pushed the girl down to the ground as it passed overhead. Seeing the landing gear down, the one-eyed man snapped, "Are we near an airport?"

"Yes, I think so. It should be just over the hill."

Ramming a fresh magazine up the butt of the Metalifed Browning, Frost grabbed her hand and shouted, "Come on! Run!"

They raced across the field and up a small hillside. The subgunners had gotten the ladder back up, Frost guessed, looking back. They were running after him and the girl.

Frost and the girl kept running, heading off across the last expanse of grass, stopping before a fence, the runways beyond it. Frost hauled himself up over the fence, helping the girl, then running with her toward a large hangar at the other end of the field where the one-eyed man could see several private planes.

In mid-stride, Frost turned and fired, aiming for the nearest of the two subgunners, hitting him and bringing the man down. Frost fired again, two two-round bursts, dropping the second man. "Search the planes for one with a key," Frost shouted to the girl as they reached the hangar. "You sure you can fly?" he shouted to her.

"Yes, dammit! I found a plane!"

Frost backed away from the hangar doors in a hail of submachinegun bullets, the second van pulling up. The girl already had the twin engine Beechcraft's engines running and was pulling away. Frost ran for it, scrambling through the open fuselage door. As he slipped into the co-pilot's seat, the Beechcraft was already pulling onto the runway. The black van was racing alongside on their right flank, the automatic weapons firing. The girl cut the plane 180 degrees, taxiing across the runway, almost straight at the van. One of the subgunners jumped out, firing, the girl cutting into the man with the starboard propeller as the plane got airborne.

Gunfire echoed behind them as they leveled off. Frost breathed a heavy sigh, saying, "I ever tell ya airplanes make me horny?" She was smiling.

Chapter 25

The sun was setting, red orange, as Frost, in Sam Kelsoe's car, and a half-dozen other cars converged on the main entrance of Dean International. Frost, Kelsoe and Felicity, each carrying riot shotguns, piled out of the lead car. Plainclothesmen and uniformed police officers emerged from the other cars, some running off to the sides of the building, others crouching behind their cars, one uniformed officer walking up to Frost and the others, carrying a bullhorn.

A SWAT team, uniformed in black baseball caps, dark coveralls and flak vests, carrying assault rifles and shotguns, stormed the front glass doors, fanning out to cover as Frost, Kelsoe and the girl moved in after them. Frost led the SWAT team into the private elevator to Dean's office, the security officer in the lobby looking baffled as Kelsoe flashed his badge and took the key to the elevator. Felicity and Kelsoe crowded into the elevator as well.

As the elevator opened to the penthouse suite, Frost dropped to one knee, tromboning the pump action of the Mossberg 500 ATP6P. The one-eyed man heard a tiny explosion, like a gun shot, coming from the receptionist's desk and opened fire, the SWAT team opening up their assault rifles, shredding the heavy looking wooden desk. As the SWAT team fanned out, Frost approached the desk and reached down into the broken pieces and picked up a tiny toy pistol with a flag coming out of the muzzle, the flag reading "BANG!" Frost, showing it to Kelsoe and the girl, before dropping it back into the rubble, smiled, "It looks like Dean has a sense of humor."

Frost followed the SWAT team into Senator Dean's office. Drawers were stacked on the desk and a wooden file cabinet stood open and empty. "Looks like Dean is going to ground," Kelsoe remarked. Frost began casually sifting through papers littered on the desk top.

"Look at this," Frost murmured, handing his police shotgun to one of the SWAT team men.

Kelsoe and Felicity walked over to the desk. Frost said, "A gas station receipt."

Felicity took it in her hand. Looking at it a moment, she said, "Just a plain old gas receipt. I've seen ones like this before—I mean from this station. Senator Dean has an experimental station in the swamps and I met him at this gas station once right after I first started working for him. It's the only station near the place and the attendant told me he always sees Dean on the way out of the swamps. Fixed a flat for him once. See, there aren't any roads leading to the station and Senator Dean keeps his swamp glider there."

Frost turned to Kelsoe, "Why don't you get onto the police down there and see if Dean's swamp boat is gone?"

Kelsoe walked around the desk and picked up the phone.

"Do you think he's gone there? It's supposed to be like a fortress."

"If he has, Felicity, I just hope we're not too far behind him."

Frost sifted through more of the papers on the desk. Kelsoe slammed down the receiver. Frost looked at him. "Let's get going; I'll get a helicopter waiting and a couple squads of Marines to meet us there. The service station attendant's body was just found, and Dean's swamp boat is missing."

Frost said nothing, but started running toward the elevator, Kelsoe and the girl on his heels.

Chapter 26

Frost, Kelsoe and the girl boarded the Coast Guard helicopter on the pad on the roof of Dean International, Kelsoe the last to come aboard, interrupted by a man in a three-piece suit and sunglasses who'd arrived aboard the chopper but now stood by on the pad.

The chopper started airborne, Frost leaning up toward Kelsoe, Kelsoe shouting something. "Phillip Piersen—not his real name. Ernest Baker. Weren't any prints on him here in the U.S. beyond the regular stuff, but checked with London, Scotland Yard. Piersen or Baker was presumed dead. That's why we didn't have a sheet on him. He killed three security guards and two bank patrons during a robbery five years ago. Police chased him—or at least they thought he was in the car with the other two men. The car ran off an embankment and exploded. They didn't find enough of the bodies for a positive identification, but witnesses in the bank gave them the description and they matched it to Pier-sen—Baker, whatever. Same man who pulled off two other bank jobs and killed four other people."

"Nice guy!" Frost shouted over the whirring of the rotors. The helicopter had swung seaward for a moment and was now heading back in-land—Frost could watch the city lights of Miami Beach below.

"That's not all—there was a man named Emil Fosberg—a PhD, one of the country's leading computer software experts. Kidnapped from his home two weeks ago! Well, once we made the prints on Piersen, it turned out a latent print at the kidnapping scene matched up."

"I don't follow you!" the girl shouted to Kelsoe.

"Easy," Frost shouted. "Piersen kidnapped this Doctor Fosberg."

"If they are after the space shuttle, Doctor Fosberg might be the link; here's his picture," and Kelsoe reached a black and white print out of his jacket pocket. Frost studied the face—sixtyish, white hair, a small beard. Frost seemed to remember you called the style an Imperial.

"Here," Frost rasped, giving Kelsoe back the picture. "If they've got Fosberg, lay ya even money he's at that base in the swamp. That's just gonna make gettin' in there that much more dif-ficult if we want to get him out alive."

"I needed this!" Kelsoe snarled.

Frost looked at Kelsoe for a second in the dashboard lights, then down to the fading lights of Miami below. In a little while they'd land and prepare for the assault on Dean's base. And now there was the kidnapped Doctor Fosberg to complicate things. "Wonderful," Frost mumured to himself. "Wonderful."

Chapter 27

On a rough wooden landing, Hank Frost stood before a swamp glider. Already aboard were two Marines in full battle gear, M-16 rifles slung on their shoulders, camouflage stick rubbed on their faces. Frost checked the magazine in the High Power.

Kelsoe walked out onto the landing, saying, "All the boats are loaded and manned, Hank."

"How many hours 'til dawn, Sam?" Frost asked.

Kelsoe checked his watch. "I make it just under two. And just after that the space shuttle will be launched from the Cape. Should make for quite a spectacular sight. We won't be so far down range that we shouldn't get a good view."

The girl, outfitted in borrowed fatigues, walked up to Frost and Kelsoe. She asked, "Do you think Dean and Eva Chapmann are planning to interfere with the guidance system of the shuttle and are trying to bring it down?"

Kelsoe answered, "I don't know what to think, but we should be there in plenty of time to stop them if they are."

Frost, lighting a cigarette, said, "I think they plan to bring it down over a populated area. Maybe Miami. It would be useless to try to figure out where—Miami, Cuba—start a war that way. But there's only one way to find out, isn't there?" Frost checked the Rolex, saying, "Let's move out" as he jumped down from the landing and onto the airboat.

Kelsoe gave him a half-salute, saying, "I'll be with the Coast Guard landing force. Good luck, Hank."

Frost smiled and looked up at Felicity as Kelsoe ran off to the waiting helicopter. Reaching up to the landing, he offered his hand to the girl. She took it and hopped aboard. He turned to the Marine at the controls. "Let's get started."

The girl looked at Frost, saying, "I guess we will find out, won't we?"

Frost didn't say anything.

Chapter 28

Mists and fog covered patches of the shallow swampwaters. Nervously, Frost eyed the armada of swamp gliders around him, alligators snapping their jaws occasionally as a boat slithered past over the water, the fan-like props whirring like a swarm of insects. Frost stood erect in the lead boat, one of the two Marines crouched beside him, an M-16 at the ready, the muzzle searching over the muddy waters. As a flock of marsh birds noisily took flight, Frost turned and looked to his left, squinting at the orange orb of light nestling above the tops of the distant mangrove trees. He brushed away a low hanging vine with his hand. Then, the girl whispered, "We're almost there, Hank. It should be around the next bend up ahead. I saw a map of the place once and the terrain matches."

Frost nodded and said to the Marine piloting the swampboat, "Look over beyond there for someplace to put to ground."

The young Marine nodded.

Giving a hand-signal to the other boats, Frost brought the armada to a ragged halt. Crouching in the prow of the swampboat, Frost rasped to the girl, "We haven't had much time to get to know one another. Maybe we can . . ."

The girl, smiling, said, "What is it that you have in mind?"

Ignoring her answer, Frost said, "Tell me something. Earlier, when we flew to the staging area in the helicopter and I was telling Kelsoe about Dean having financed Eva Chapmann's father, you seemed to know as much about it as I did. Did you know Marcus Chapmann?"

"Don't be silly, how would I know a—"

Frost cut her off, "A mercenary? You know me, right? Did you know him? Answer me!" Frost put his hands on her arms; she turned her face away, but then turned back to look up at him.

"Yes. Marcus Chapmann murdered my fiance." Her voice dropped and she said, "Yes—are you happy now?" She glared at him.

"No—as a matter of fact I'm not." Looking at her, Frost rasped, "I'm sorry for you. I know it doesn't help, but I'm still sorry."

The swamp glider lurched to a stop against a muddy spot, drier land visible on the far side. Clapping the Marine pilot on the shoulder, Frost said, "Have the others spread out in a line. Pole the boats, after I get off until you get just around the bend over there."

The Marine signaled with his hands and the

swampboats started to line up on Frost's boat, keeping it in the center of the line. Frost, the mists rolling in tiny clouds past his face, checked the M-16, then his Metalifed Browning, taking it from his shoulder holster. Holding the assault rifle, Frost started to put his combat-booted right foot over the side of the swamp glider.

"You don't have to go alone, Hank," the girl said, touching at Frost's left shoulder.

He turned and smiled at her. "Too many men would alert them. I've got to see where they're holding Doctor Fosberg before the assault begins."

"Hank," the girl said, touching at his shoulder again, then touching her hand to his cheek, "I must sound—but I do care—" Cutting herself off, she hastily kissed him on the mouth. Frost glanced at the young Marine, watching them.

Smiling, Frost stepped overboard and waded through the shallow water toward the muddy spot of land. The Marine piloting his air boat said, "Good luck, sir."

Sidestepping a water moccasin, his stomach churning just seeing it, Frost crossed onto the land, moving into the trees for cover. He broke across a small clearing then and dropped down behind a log. The buildings of the research station were in view in the distance. Frost looked over the top of the log, the rifle in front of him, his chin resting on the receiver. He thought he could just make out guards walking from between two of the buildings, SMGs slung on their shoulders. "Wonderful," he murmured.

Chapter 29

The old buildings themselves were pre-
fabricated metal structures and some older
wooden shacks. A long jetty ran out from the
cluster of buildings into the river in the distance,
the river as wide as if it were a lake. Aside from
the guards, no other activity was noticeable.

Frost pushed himself up and took off at a dead
run across the open expanse before him to the
nearest building, flattening himself against its
ridged aluminum side. As he started to move out,
the one-eyed man froze. A guard was walking
round the corner of the building. Frost crushed
the back of the man's skull with the butt of his
M-16. Awkwardly because of the soft ground and
the man's weight, Frost dragged him under the
building's framework, into a crawlspace area.

Getting out from under the building, Frost,
keeping to a low crouch, ran toward the next
building. He risked a look through the rain-
spattered window. Frost saw no one. He tried the

153

lock; then slowly opened the metal door, the muzzle of the M-16 ahead of him, and cautiously stepped inside.

The building was quiet and lit well from the rising sun behind him, despite the dirty windows. Frost walked across the board floor, passing through beams of sunlight from the windows, and stopped at the far wall. Frost wheeled, the door in the wall beside him opening, some of Dean's and Eva Chapmann's men starting through. Frost slammed the door into the face of the first man, then darted to the center of the room, shooting the second and third men as they plowed through the doorway. Frost raced toward the entrance door through which he'd come. A shotgun blast ripped into the door as he started to reach for it. Frost turned and fired again, hitting the man carrying the riot shotgun squarely in the body and knocking him halfway across the room from the impact of the 5.56 mm burst.

Frost pushed through the door, outside. In the distance, he could hear the swamp glider armada roaring toward the research station, drawn by the gunfire. Out of the huts were pouring dozens of men armed with submachineguns and riot shotguns.

Frost raced from the building and across the compound, shooting out the thirty-round mag in the M-16, ramming a fresh one home. On the far side of the research station, he could see the swamp gliders landing. At the jetty now, Frost saw one of Dean's and Eva Chapmann's men trying to pull away in an Avon inflatable boat. Frost fired a burst from the M-16, hitting the motor, the boat exploding, throwing the man high into the air, the body aflame. Frost wheeled, using the long barrel of the assault rifle to rake a riot shotgun-carrying man across the face.

There was a small hut at the far end of the jetty. A dozen of Dean's and Chapmann's men were shooting it out with Marines from the swamp glider force. Frost fought his way toward the hut, killing three men rushing him from the land side. Gone half the length of the jetty now, Frost, his M-16 empty, jumped off the pier into one of the Avon boats, a man with a subgun trying to escape in it. Using the butt of his M-16, Frost smashed the man in the side of the head, hurtling the man back, overboard. Throwing the M-16 into the bottom of the boat, Frost turned the craft toward the head of the jetty and the hut where the fighting still raged. Off in the distance, Frost could see Coast Guard cutters coming up the river—"Kelsoe!"

Frost hugged the rubber boat close to the jetty, but some of Dean's and Eva Chapmann's men had apparently spotted him now, opening fire. Frost's boat was hit, again and again, starting to lose air. Frost jumped clear, onto the pylons supporting the jetty. And underneath the jetty, the one-eyed man spotted several large fuel drums, stacked just at the water level. Frost started to climb along the pylons, toward the hut above him, but stopped. There was a man on the far side of the fuel drums.

Frost, working his way across and around the

drums, could see the man clearly now, striking a match, lighting it to a fuse. Frost's eye followed the fuse. It stopped at two cases, two cases marked "Dynamite" nested in the center of the fuel drums.

Frost clambered across the fuel drums toward the fuse, slipping, falling, but moving again. The man who'd lit the fuse had spotted him. The man dove toward Frost now, jumping at Frost with a bayonet. Frost caught the knife hand wrist, rolling back across the oil drums and into the water.

The fuse was still burning.

In the water now, near the fuel drums, the man lunged at Frost, the bayonet slicing the air inches from Frost's face. The man lunged again, the drag of the water slowing him. Frost blocked it, catching the wrist of the man's knife arm with his right hand. Frost elbowed him in the jaw, twisting the wrist, getting the knife away and thrusting it hard into the man's throat. Frost pushed the dead man away, leaving the body to float off on the water.

Frost's own knife in his teeth now, the one-eyed man climbed onto the fuel drums, the end of the fuse now burnt down to where he couldn't reach it. From above him, over the noise of gunfire, Frost heard a sound he couldn't mistake—a man's scream. Jumping onto one of the wooden pylons, Frost used the ropes bound around it like a ladder, scaling the pylon to reach the jetty. Pulling himself up and over the side, Frost sidestepped, one of Dean's and Chapmann's men diving toward him. Frost feigned a punch, then made a low kick to the groin, pushing the man over the side and into the water.

Reaching the door of the hut, Frost heard another scream, muffled now. The one-eyed man kicked open the door. Inside the hut, lying on a cot on the far side of the room, his head bandaged, was Doctor Fosberg, the missing software expert. One of Dean's and Chapmann's men, an SMG slung over his shoulder, was smothering Fosberg with a pillow. Framed in the doorway, snatching the knife from his teeth as he spoke, Frost called out, "Behind you!"

As the man turned, his SMG coming to bear, Frost tossed the little Gerber knife underhand, nailing the man squarely in the chest. Frost raced to the cot, grabbing his knife and snatching up the old man into his arms. Then he made for the door.

Through the doorway, Frost ran the few feet toward the edge then jumped from the jetty and into the water, the old man still in his arms. As they hit the water, Frost fought to hold the man's head above it. An Avon boat was starting past them, with one of Dean's and Chapmann's men aboard. Letting go of the old man a moment, Frost grabbed onto the side of the boat and, pulling himself aboard, jumped the man. The one-eyed man kneed the man in the crotch, tossing him overboard.

Frost reached over the side of the rubber boat, hauling in the old man. Dr. Fosberg only half in the boat, Frost glanced down at his watch, then gave the outboard motor full throttle. As the boat lurched under him out into the river, the dynamite in the fuel dump blew, the gasoline igniting and the entire jetty and the hut disintegrating. Flames leaped high into the air, the heat searing Frost's face. . . .

Frost could see Sam Kelsoe, standing in the prow of a Coast Guard cutter, hailing him. As soon as Frost got the boat near enough, a hook was put out, bringing him alongside. Frost climbed aboard. As Doctor Fosberg was carried past, Frost studied the face—still alive.

Frost walked over to Kelsoe, who offered Frost a cigarette. Another Avon boat heaved to beside the cutter; Felicity Grey was helped aboard. As she walked over, she said to Frost, "I saw what you did—saving the life of Doctor Fosberg. You're a brave man."

"Look at that," Kelsoe shouted and Frost turned. A sound like thunder. Louder, growing in intensity. The massive shape of the space shuttle, mounted against the still more massive external tank and solid boosters. A tongue of flame following it. Kelsoe turned to clap Frost on the back, but the girl was already kissing him. As the sound of the launch died, Frost could hear the Marines and Coast Guardsmen cheering.

Chapter 30

Hank Frost's head was resting on a pillow, his eye closed. He moved his hand almost angrily to brush something away from his face. The girl laughed and leaned over him as he opened his eye, taking the end of a wisp of brown hair and tickling him in the ear. Frost grabbed her into his arms. On his back, the girl resting on his chest, Frost smiled, "I think we're doing this upside down."

She laughed. Frost kissed her hard on the mouth, rolling her over in the bed. The girl cradled in his left arm, he looked down at her, resting on his right elbow, saying, "Feeling better?"

"Uh-huh," she groaned in his ear. As Frost kissed her neck and she moved in his arms, she whispered, "Better and better . . . and better . . ."

The telephone rang and Frost looked at it angrily, then reached out for the receiver and slowly took it from the cradle. Rolling onto his back, the girl twisting the cord in her fingers, Frost spoke into the receiver, saying, "Yes?"

The girl watched him intently as Frost said, "All right, Sam, we'll be right there." Frost leaned across the girl to hang up the phone and, as he did, she wrapped her arms around his neck.

"What did Kelsoe want, Hank?"

"Doctor Fosberg seems to be waking up—coming out of the coma. Seems that Sam feels Fosberg may be able to answer some questions. We have no idea what state his mind is in or what they did to him. Maybe, he can give us a clue as to where Eva Chapmann and Senator Dean went, or what they plan next." She rolled over on her stomach, her lips set in a pout. Frost smacked her lightly on the rear end and she turned to face him. He kissed her on the mouth. "Come on." He smacked her again on the rear end, harder, rolling out of bed . . .

Frost, then Felicity after him, stepped out of the back seat of the Lincoln towncar and turned to look up at the hospital, towering over the street. The girl beside him, he walked to the main entrance and passed inside, stopping for a moment at the elevator bank, then entering a car. Elevators still made him nervous. As the doors opened, Frost and the girl stepped out, following two nurses talking to one another animatedly. Sam Kelsoe called out to them, "Over here, Hank!"

Frost and the girl walked up to the nurses' station where Kelsoe said, "Hank, this is Doctor Smallwood. Doctor, this is Hank Frost and Felicity Grey."

Frost, shaking hands with the white coated man said, "Doctor, a pleasure."

The doctor, as if continuing a conversation, said, "He was badly shaken, lost a lot of blood and that scalp wound was a deep one. He was in deep shock and he's only just come out of it. I realize the importance of this from what you told me, Mr. Kelsoe, what you were able to tell me. But only one or two questions. If Doctor Fosberg appears straining to answer you, we'll have to stop. It would be too easy for him to lapse back into a coma. And we don't want to lose him."

The doctor leading the way, Frost, Kelsoe and the girl followed him down the corridor. Outside the room—a sign on the door saying 'Authorized Admittance Only'—were members of the Miami SWAT team. Kelsoe nodded and Frost, Kelsoe and the girl followed the doctor inside. A nurse was at the bedside. Frost and the girl stood by the door. Kelsoe looked at the doctor and the doctor nodded. Kelsoe cautiously approached the bed. A myriad of tubes led from Doctor Fosberg's body to bottles and vials suspended round the bed like decorations. A heart monitor was connected to the old man and Kelsoe looked over his shoulder as it electronically echoed Fosberg's heart rate on a screen behind him. Kelsoe turned to Fosberg, bending very close to him, saying, "Doctor Fosberg. This is Sam Kelsoe—FBI. You're all right now. You're in a hospital in Miami guarded by the police. But we need to know where Senator Dean and Eva Chapmann have gone. And what they plan with that guidance equipment. Can you hear me?''

The old man's eyes opened and he looked about the room. His eyes stopped on Frost and he mumbled feebly, ''You—saved—my life . . .'' Then his eyes turned to Kelsoe. ''North. Manhattan . . .'' Then his head lolled over. The doctor rushed up to Fosberg and turned to check the instruments. He turned to Kelsoe and then to Frost and the girl, saying, ''It's all right. He's just fallen asleep. I think he's going to make it.'' The doctor started for the door, Frost and the others following him through.

Walking partway down the hall, they stopped and Kelsoe said, ''What did you think he meant?''

''I think he just gave us a target, Sam,'' Frost mused.

Chapter 31

Frost, Felicity Grey and Sam Kelsoe sat around the small conference table in a large room in the Federal Building. Frost took off his jacket, the Metalifed High Power in the shoulder rig under his left arm.

"Let me see that gun of yours—you mind?"

"What?" Frost looked absently at Kelsoe.

"Your gun, that finish looks good. O'Hara's is like that, isn't it?"

"Yeah; that big Model 29 of his," Frost noted, ripping the Browning from the leather, dumping the magazine and jacking back the slide to clear the chamber. He passed the gun to Felicity who sat between them, then she in turn passed it to Kelsoe.

"Who does this?" Kelsoe asked.

"Ron Mahovsky—old buddy of mine. Mostly does revolvers, but he'll do automatics too. Should have had him out there at that base Dean had in the swamps; hell of a good man with a gun, terrific at martial arts."

"What do you think's their next move?" Felicity Grey asked.

"Well," Frost murmured, lighting a Camel. "Before we figure that out, I think it's about time you gave us the whole shot on what you know about Eva Chapmann, how the death of your fiance got you working for Creighton Dean; little stuff like that, kid. I don't wanna stir up any bad memories, but we gotta know."

He watched her dark eyes a moment, then she looked down into her hands. "Would you believe Dean's an Equal Opportunity Employer, Male-Female?"

"No," Frost said flatly.

"Didn't think you would. It's a long story."

"Since we don't know what Eva Chapmann and Creighton Dean's next moves are, have no place to go—I guess I got the time."

"All right, Hank," she said, her eyes hard-looking to Frost. "Dean had financed Marcus Chapmann through some blind accounts a couple of times. My fiance—Dan Ormsby—found that out in Africa. He was with CIA there. Well, Dan apparently figured he was really getting close. He was stateside for a few weeks and this one night, well—he got drunk and he talked. I knew he wasn't supposed to, and I wasn't supposed to listen, but I let him talk. I could see something had been bothering him. You know—an ex-Senator, a rich and powerful man like Creighton Dean mixed up with a mercenary like Chapmann."

"There are mercs like Chapmann, but most of them aren't," Frost interjected. "Don't bad mouth my profession."

"Let her finish, huh?" Kelsoe said.

Frost nodded.

Clearing her throat, Felicity Grey went on, "Well, anyway, I heard it all. I didn't tell him. Maybe I should have. He went back to Africa and three weeks later they found his body. They never gave me the details. I was going to try to find a way to do something about Chapmann; but somebody had killed him."

"Me," Frost said, emotionlessly.

The girl looked at him, and so did Kelsoe.

"But when I found out he was dead, I decided to try to get Creighton Dean. I asked CIA through channels if they knew what Dan had been working on before he died—they wouldn't tell me. So it had to be Dean, I figured. I decided the best way to get to Dean was to join him. A secretarial job or something wouldn't have gotten me close to him. Dan had taught me how to shoot a handgun and some martial arts stuff. And I read an article about Dean International Security in some magazine. So, I got into a martial arts program, went to the range four times a week, made myself so good, Dean would have to hire me. And he did—at least Phillip Piersen did. I've been trying to pick up bits and pieces on Dean ever since."

"He must have figured you were; that's why he set you up with me when those guys came at us on the road to his ranch."

"But he kept me working for him anyway?"

Kelsoe interrupted. "Sometimes, you get a mole in your outfit—somebody you can't trust and you keep around, just in case you need to feed somebody the wrong information some time. It's easy enough to isolate somebody from the important stuff when you have to. That's probably what Dean did."

"Dammit," she snapped.

Frost looked at her, not able to help himself, laughing. "Well—at least you're alive."

"But I did find out he was supplying funds to some account in Switzerland, then the money would get withdrawn and he'd put in more. That must have been Eva Chapmann."

"Probably," Kelsoe said. "We're trying to run some checks, but Swiss bankers—"

"Look—God bless 'em," Frost smiled.

"Okay; what have we got?" Kelsoe began.

"A conference table, three people—"

"Dammit, Frost," Kelsoe snarled.

"Couldn't pass it up," the one-eyed man laughed.

"Let's try to piece together something. Okay?" Kelsoe asked.

Frost nodded and so did the girl.

"All right then—they kidnapped Doctor Fosberg, made the attempt to get the two of you on the way out to Dean's ranch. Fosberg is one of the leading computer software experts in the country. All that electronic equipment out at the base in the swamps. But they were killing Doctor Fosberg."

"So," Frost chimed in. "That was just a temporary base. They used Fosberg to make a software program for them and then Chapmann and Dean left—along with Piersen. They would kill Fosberg to make sure he didn't tell anybody what kind of program he'd made for them."

"And Fosberg mentioned Manhattan," Felicity added.

"North and Manhattan," Frost corrected. "If we assume this is all tied into the space shuttle, what could north, Manhattan and a software program have to—"

"And Dean Guidance Systems—don't forget that," Kelsoe added.

"Wait a minute," the girl almost gasped. "Dean had about five thousand shares of different New York Stock Exchange listed commodities sold about a week ago. I thought maybe he needed investment capital or something."

"Naw," Frost moaned.

"What?" Kelsoe asked.

"It's like something out of some crazy spy movie."

"What?" Kelsoe insisted.

Frost shrugged. "Okay—I'll whip it on you. But don't laugh too loud. What if Creighton Dean manufactured compatible computer hardware with the guidance equipment NASA uses to remotely control the space shuttle? And what if he forced Fosberg to write him a program that would override NASA and allow Dean and Eva Chapmann to control the ship from the ground? And what if right now, they're setting up to course correct the shuttle and bring it down—but like a rock—right in the middle of Manhattan?"

"You're right—that's crazy," Kelsoe said.

"No—all those stocks he sold. Those were Manhattan based companies. If the shuttle crashed there, why—all their corporate records would be destroyed, the companies would—"

"That's stupid; there isn't enough fuel aboard the shuttle to do all that. Maybe destroy a couple of city blocks—"

"Right in the financial district," she added.

"Naw—it's a dumb idea," Frost insisted.

"Do you remember the names of those companies Dean sold out of?" Kelsoe asked.

"I think so."

"You mean," Frost rasped, "that if all the corporate headquarters are in the same couple of blocks, we've got ground zero?"

"Maybe," Kelsoe said slowly.

"But what would he have to gain?" Frost said.

"Before we tipped to him," Felicity answered, "he stood a lot to gain. Dean was heavily invested in the European space shuttle program through dummy companies; that's another piece of information I picked up. If our space shuttle destroyed part of New York, regardless of the circumstances, it would put NASA out of business and make the European space shuttle program the only way to go. Dean would have made millions, maybe billions."

Frost just looked at her, saying nothing for a moment; then: "And now he's just doing it for revenge—ohh, hell!"

"Give me that list of companies," Kelsoe said.

Chapter 32

"I got no choice, Frost—I could write you in before because we needed you to flush out Dean. And then that assault on Dean's Research Station in the swamps—there wasn't time for the Bureau to kill your being in on it. But you and Felicity are civilians; so I gotta tell you to stay out of it."

"Bullshit!" The girl shrieked. "I gave you the information on those companies in New York, let you find out what Dean's ground zero was, let you figure the whole thing and—"

"Shut up," Frost snapped, not looking at the girl as he said it, but looking at Sam Kelsoe. He said to Kelsoe, "Have you got a line on where they could be setting up?"

"I'm not supposed to tell you anything," Kelsoe said, sitting down behind his desk.

"That's not what I asked," Frost growled.

"All right—but you didn't hear it from me. I had a hard time talking 'em out of putting you and her under protective custody until this was all over."

"Where, Sam?" Frost insisted.

"We don't know yet—probably somewhere in western Pennsylvania, eastern Ohio. That'd give them enough time to intercept the shuttle with their electronics and start it on a controlled descent to drop it down in the Big Apple."

"Western Pennsylvania, or maybe eastern Ohio—terrific." Frost looked at the girl as he stood up. "Come on, Felicity—buy you a drink at the airport."

"Where are you going?" Kelsoe demanded.

Frost turned around and grinned at him. "I hear Cleveland is lovely this time of year."

"Frost!"

Frost looked over his shoulder at Kelsoe. "Sam—you're Mike O'Hara's friend, you been okay to me; but if you and your guys try stoppin' me from going up there, looking for Eva Chapmann and this Dean creep myself, well—I never shot at FBI guys before, but I guess I can start."

"Frost—"

"What?" the one-eyed man snapped.

"Good luck—but don't tell anybody I said it." Kelsoe grinned. So did Frost.

Chapter 33

Frost listened to the telephone ringing, waiting for someone to answer it.

"Mahovsky's," the voice on the other end of the line said.

"Ron?" This is Hank Frost."

"Frost? Gee, man—where are ya'?"

"You believe Cleveland?"

"Cleveland? Why hell, you're less than—"

"I know—I'm plannin' on it. Wanted to see if you could help me out, make a few calls for me?" Frost said.

"What's up, man?"

"I'm lookin' for information on somebody maybe not too far from you—settin' up some kind of a base—"

"A base? What are you into, Frost?"

"Naw—hear me out. A lot of guys—maybe visibly armed. Don't know. Probably some trucks to get in some heavy equipment—electronics stuff. Probably some kind of antenna—like a T.V.

earthstation, only maybe larger, maybe two of them."

"What's coming down, man?"

"Not on the phone; but if we find it, you wanna help?"

"Yeah—hey. Count me in, huh. I been loadin' up .45 ACP the last coupla months and me and my boy been loading .223—yeah, count me in."

"Take me a couple hours—gonna have a girl with me—Felicity Grey."

"Fine; don't look for a motel. We'll put you up. Hey, what do I do if I fine something?"

"Keep it until I get there," Frost said into the phone. "Get all the poop you can on it and we'll go from there."

"Gotchya—hey, listen."

"Yeah," Frost said.

"We find whatever you're lookin' for—well, hell I got these trailbikes. We can boogie on up there and—sounds like fun."

Frost shook his head at the receiver and laughed. "You haven't changed—see ya."

He turned to Felicity Grey, standing behind him outside the phone booth. "Who was that?" she asked.

"Old buddy of mine—you'll love him."

"Where are we going?"

"A cabin in the woods in Pennsylvania—at least for openers," and Frost, his hands reaching down for his flight bag and the gray plastic pistol case and the Safariland SWAT bag, started walking. . . .

Chapter 34

The dirt road was still rutted, from the last heavy rains Frost supposed, and ahead of him now, in a sort of valley, he could see Mahovsky's "cabin." Frost's gunsmithing friend had built the house himself from logs, carefully gauging each step in the building process to keep the logs from shifting once in place and to make them seal together properly. With his wife and son and daughter, Mahovsky had a wilderness retreat—Frost envied him for it.

Frost parked the rented Ford LTD in front of the house, starting to get out. He turned around, hearing the familiar voice behind him. "You really got yourself into something, didn't you," Mahovsky smiled.

Frost looked at the tall, lean man, then grinned. "I guess you got some information, pal."

"Yeah—kinda. Who's the lady?"

Frost glanced over his shoulder, across the roofline of the LTD at Felicity Grey. "Felicity

Grey, meet Ron Mahovsky. Ron, Felicity. That's all taken care of."

"Hank didn't tell me about the beard—I like beards," she smiled.

"Yeah, well—betchya he didn't tell you a lot of things about me—ha," and Mahovsky walked across the drive toward the car. He stretched out his right hand, Frost taking it.

"Carol and the kids are away; maybe just as well with what I found out," Mahovsky grinned. "Good thing I was loadin' all that .223 and .45 ACP, man. I did some checkin' around—you know. Well, I think I found what you want. Come on inside."

Frost looked across the car at Felicity; there was an odd look in her eyes. If the one-eyed man hadn't known better, he would have thought it was happiness, a sudden relaxation of tension. He mentally shrugged. Maybe it was all of that—killing Creighton Dean was something she seemed to need to do. . . .

Cabin on the outside, Mahovsky's house was just as Frost remembered it—comfortable, spacious and modern on the inside. They sat, the three of them, in the kitchen, around a wooden table, Frost drinking decaffeinated coffee—the only kind Mahovsky kept in the house—and Felicity drinking orange juice. Mahovsky was pouring hot water into a cup; then he set the kettle down on the stove and sat down. "So—tell me about these guys. I think I found 'em for ya, you know."

"Well—you ever hear me mention Marcus

Chapmann—Colonel Marcus Chapmann?''

''Yeah—that was that sucker you smoked after he massacred all your people down in—where the hell was it?''

''Down in South America—yeah, that was him,'' Frost nodded. ''Well—he had a daughter. She was raised in Germany. Don't know much more about her, really. Chapmann kept a picture of her on his desk, whenever he had a desk. Well—looks like she took over her dad's old business.''

''Mercenaries?''

''Yeah—but there are mercenaries and then there are mercenaries—she's just like her father. Looks like she put together some kind of crew nobody in his right mind would hire.''

''Well, that explains that. Maybe she isn't in her right mind, you know?''

''Yeah, anyway, she set up this phony reunion down in South Africa. Got me down there, put the bag on me. Woke up goin' blind in the jungle. Tracked down her guys, got myself the right injection and counteracted whatever the hell it was she'd had 'em give me. Stopped some of her guys raping a young native girl, found out her father and a bunch of the guys in his village were just as angry at Eva Chapmann as I was. She'd been lettin' her guys grab their women and the girls had been turning up dead—''

''She's gotta be sick, you know?''

Frost nodded to his friend. ''Anyway—there was a fight at her house—big, fortified place. But she got away. Trail led me to Florida, town called

Morrison. She either had wires on me and knew I was coming or somebody spotted me. I don't know. Two guys tried killing me in my hotel room."

"Why Morrison, Florida? Never heard of the place."

"She must have had some kind of safe house down there—there was a big shootout between some of her guys smuggling weapons into the country and the FBI. That pal of mine, Mike O'Hara?"

"O'Hara—wait a minute," Mahovsky said thoughtfully. "Kind of loudmouthed guy—talks weird?"

"Yeah—"

"I did a gun for him. A 29, I think it was. Wouldn't let me round the butt, but I chamfered all the charging holes in the cylinder, rounded the rear sight blade, gave him a smooth trigger, did an action job, nice polishing job then I Metalifed it. Shoulda let me round the butt, you know? Cuts the recoil—at least the way you feel it."

"Yeah; well O'Hara got shot-up. Last I heard he was still in a coma. So Chapmann was operating from around there. I'd picked up the name Creighton Dean—"

"Wasn't he some kinda politician?"

"Yeah—among other things. She was tied in with him. A buddy of O'Hara's—Sam Kelsoe—set me up to draw out Dean by getting next to his daughter—"

"Sandra?" Felicity asked, surprised.

"Yeah—you know her?" Frost smiled.

176

"That bitch. Yeah, I know her. You're lucky she didn't suck your blood out. She's—ugghh—"

"Well—I went up to Boston, arranged an accident where I met her. Like clockwork, she made a pass at me—you believe it?" Frost smiled, lighting a cigarette. "I mean crazy. So—she set me up. Bunch of Chapmann's guys—or maybe her father's—tried killing me. Whole big gunfight along the coast there. Hey—you gotta try this Hawk MM-1; you would love it," Frost smiled.

"What is it?"

"Twelve shot repeater—grenade launcher."

"Holy—yeah, I could dig up on somethin' like that. Then what happened?"

"I got in touch with Kelsoe and we went back to Miami. I walked in on Dean—figured he'd have to know something was wrong with his daughter when I was still alive and he'd have to know who I was because he was working with Eva Chapmann—they call her the Deathwitch."

"Deathwitch, huh," Mahovsky repeated. "Well, I got the medicine right here to drive a stake into her heart—ha—you know?"

Frost started to laugh. He looked at Felicity, "You see why I called Mahovsky—having him with us is gonna be like—"

"Hey—what can I say? So what happened next?"

"That friend of yours gonna call with where those hunters saw that satellite dish?"

Mahovsky reached across the table, turning Frost's wrist over a minute to read Frost's watch. "Yeah—give 'em five minutes more. Chako's goin' up there, you know—gonna call in to his kid brother on the CB. Out of range for me here. Then the kid'll call me. We should know in five minutes or so. But what happened?"

"Frost met me at Dean's offices; I was working for Dean—"

"Working for him?"

"She was trying to get something on him. See, Felicity's fiance—guy named Dan, right?" and Frost looked at the girl. She only nodded. "Well—Dan was tracking down a connection between Creighton Dean and Marcus Chapmann. Dan was killed, over in Africa," and Frost looked at the girl again. She just nodded. "Then I smoked Marcus Chapmann. So Felicity went after Creighton Dean. Dean had apparently gotten wise to her. See, I walked in there with this fakey CIA ID and Dean knew who I was all the time, but couldn't knock me off—not there—"

"Are you the guy who put Chup Teng in the hospital? See, that's where I heard about Dean before—I knew I remembered it."

Frost looked at Mahovsky, mystified.

"Look," Mahovsky smiled. Frost watched as Mahovsky took a packet of decaffeinated coffee and sprinkled a few granules into the hot water, barely coloring it, then lifted the cup and sipped at it.

"How can you drink that stuff so weak?" the girl asked.

"I just color my hot water. Too much caffeine's bad for you, you know? But anyway, I think you and me are the only guys who ever took

178

Chup Teng. He was up in Cleveland couple of years ago. Some friends of mine and I were up there, you know? Well, Chup Teng spotted my buddy was in martial arts and started baitin' him. Two of 'em went out into the parking lot. Chup Teng pounded my buddy into the concrete. Well, you know, that was fine, all fair and everything, right? But then Chup Teng started poundin' on him when he was unconscious. I told him to knock it off, see? Well, he told me to make him. So, I peeled off my coat and my gun and—well, I made him. See, I used this kick routine I started workin' into my kata—you know? Slammed that sucker right into the trunk of a Lincoln—man, was he gone. Wish somebody'd had a camera. But see, all the stuff that happens in the martial arts gets around. I heard about Chup Teng windin' up in the hospital from a buddy of mine down in Miami the other night. Did good, Frost."

"Thanks," the one-eyed man smiled.

"So what happened after you got outa Dean's place?"

"Dean asked me to take Hank out to his ranch where the shootout had been between Eva Chapmann's men and the FBI. Probably Piersen was in on that."

"Piersen?" Mahovsky asked the girl.

"Englishman—turned out he's killed at least nine people over there in bank jobs," Frost added. "He was probably the one leading the guys who tried getting us on the highway."

"What?"

"They followed us. There was a big fight," the

179

girl said, without elaborating.

"Well, after the fight," Frost went on, "we raided Dean's offices. He was gone. He and Piersen had gone down into the swamps. And then we found out Piersen had snatched some guy named Emil Fosberg—"

"The computer man? Yeah, I read an article about him," Mahovsky interjected.

"Well, they had Fosberg down at this base in the swamps and everything pointed to Dean and Chapmann doing something with the space shuttle—some kind of sabotage. We got in there, but Dean, Piersen and Chapmann were gone already. I stopped some joker trying to smother Fosberg and the shuttle got off. Later on, Fosberg regained consciousness a little and clued us to the word 'Manhattan.' Turned out Dean had sold a lot of stock in companies with their corporate headquarters within a three square block area in Manhattan. Turned out also Dean owns a lot of interest in the European space shuttle program. Looks like he and Eva Chapmann were going to use some software program Doctor Fosberg made with Dean's own guidance equipment to override the guidance controls of the space shuttle—drop it right into downtown Manhattan in the rush hour—today, tomorrow, I don't know when. But within the next five days."

The muscles around Mahovsky's eyes tightened. "You didn't have the radio on in the car, huh?"

"Why?" Frost asked, leaning forward, stubbing out his cigarette. "Why?"

"Well, I forget what they call the things—but

it's one of their power converters, you know? Total malfunction. So they're bringing the space shuttle down this evening. About six P.M.—and they got weather problems in California and at White Sands, so it'll be coming down in Florida."

Frost looked at the Rolex, Mahovsky already starting to his feet, picking up the telephone. It was three P.M.

"Hello—Jim? Ron Mahovsky, how ya doin'?. . . . You sure, Jim? What did Chako say?" Mahovsky just nodded into the phone, then said, "Sorry man—yeah, we'll look. No—we'll take care of the police."

Mahovsky hung up the phone and turned to face Frost and the girl. "Chako called Jim a couple of minutes ago. Told Jim he'd been shot and was dying. See, Jim, Chako's kid brother? He's in a wheelchair. Has been for a long time. Jim got the poop from Chako before he died—the CB just went out. Checked out that earthstation dish? Three guys with submachineguns jumped him, shot him. Guess they figured he was dead. But he crawled back to his jeep and called in."

"If the shuttle's landing around six P.M., we've got less than three hours—"

Frost interrupted the girl. "Ron and I'll go up there—Ron can pinpoint it on a map for you as best as possible while I get my boots and stuff. You stay on Ron's horn here until you get hold of Kelsoe and give him the location."

"But what if—"

"Then Chapmann and Dean win—we lose," Frost murmured.

Chapter 35

Frost slowed the borrowed trail bike, stopping it beside Mahovsky. Both men were ready for war. The odds on Kelsoe getting his people into the remote back country area where Chako had sighted the earth station dish and the three men had shot him were good; but the odds on Kelsoe getting in there much before six P.M. were bad. Frost glanced at his watch. It was already past four P.M.

Both Frost and Mahovsky carried. Interdynamics KG-9s slung diagonally cross-body under their right arms, Frost having introduced Mahovsky to the 9mm assault pistol. Mahovsky had loaned Frost an AR-15, Mahovsky with one as well. Frost had cleaned out his friend on 9mm Parabellums, all except what Mahovsky himself was using for his KG-9. Frost's Browning was in the Alessi shoulder rig under his left arm. Mahovsky, not an automatic man for years, was carrying his pet revolver, one he'd made himself. It had started as a standard Smith & Wesson Model 25-2, long barreled in .45 ACP. Mahovsky had cut the barrel back to two and three-quarter inches, crowned the muzzle, shaped the front of the ejector rod shroud, added a crane lock, round butted the gun down from N-frame to K-frame size, action tuned it—his usual job for precision combat revolvers. Using half-moon clips, the revolver reloaded almost as fast as an autoloader like Frost's High Power, and Mahovsky was lethally good with it.

But guns would be their last resort. Frost judged between Eva Chapmann's men and Dean's men under Phillip Piersen, there would be perhaps as many as a hundred. To start shooting against those odds was insanity. Both men had agreed the only chance they had of penetrating the area sufficiently to get to the guidance equipment and neutralize it was to kill their way in as silently as possible.

"I make it we've got another hour on the trail, more or less," Mahovsky told Frost.

"Then we recon the place fast," the one-eyed man answered, "but not too fast. Should leave us less than forty-five minutes before they'd take control of the space shuttle."

"Nothin' like cuttin' it thin, huh," Mahovsky laughed.

Frost looked at the man, nodding. "Yeah—I wouldn't wanna get there and have nothing to do, time to kill." Frost looked at the Rolex again. It would be time to kill in just about an hour.

Chapter 36

Frost looked westward across the low ridge from where he and Mahovsky for the last ten minutes had been studying the shallow, dish-shaped valley. The sun was lowering on the horizon. Frost glanced at his Rolex—it was five-fifteen. He didn't know much about space shuttles, or aircraft in general really. But he guessed in another fifteen minutes, if what ex-Senator Creighton Dean and Eva Chapmann had could really work, they'd take over the guidance for the shuttle. Maybe twenty-five minutes at the outside. And given the speed at which the shuttle flew, by six PM a couple of blocks in downtown Manhattan would be like a bombed zone in a war.

If the guidance equipment took over, no matter how hard the shuttle pilots would try, it would be impossible to control the craft, even just for ditching it in the ocean.

"Wanna go?" Mahovsky asked, looking at Frost.

"No—but I gotta," Frost smiled.

Frost had counted twenty-five men milling about near the massive earth-station-like radio dish. But this was for sending, not receiving. There were more men near the three red semi-trailer trucks parked in a crude circle around the dish. In one of them too would be the master controls for Dean's guidance equipment. The computers were where Doctor Fosberg's software would run, enabling Dean to override the NASA controls.

Which truck, Frost wondered.

"What?"

"I didn't say anything," Frost murmured. "Leave the AR-15s here—too bulky."

"I agree—this is knife work—knives and these," and Mahovsky gestured with his hands.

Frost only nodded, slipping the little boot knife from inside the waistband of his trousers.

Mahovsky's knife was already in his right fist, the butt of the knife—a massive lockblade folder with a five inch blade—just barely protruding from the top of his fist.

"Let's go," Frost rasped, unlimbering the AR-15 and setting it on the ground beside Mahovsky's.

Frost pushed himself up to his feet and started into a dead run, crouching as he moved toward the lip of the ridge, then half dove, half rolled below the ridgeline, skidding down the grade on his rear end and back before he got a purchase, dug in his boot heels.

Mahovsky was beside him. "Rough on the blue

jeans, ya know?'' Mahovsky observed. Frost nodded, both men starting down the grade and toward the shallow valley.

There were men, men with assault rifles and submachineguns, ringing the base at wide intervals by the tree line.

Frost could see the nearest man ahead, and started toward him.

Mahovsky grabbed Frost's arm, shaking his head, then smiling.

Frost nodded, watching Mahovsky.

Mahovsky started forward in a low crouch, rising to full height, seeming to suck air into his lungs, to inflate his chest, the tendons in the sides of his neck standing out.

Mahovsky, totally silently, was standing less than a yard behind the guard. Mahovsky's left hand reached out, gently it seemed to Frost watching him, tapping the man on the right shoulder. The man slowly—then suddenly more quickly—started to turn, Mahovsky's right fist shooting forward in a straight line to the man's adam's apple, like a piston more than a human hand.

The butt of the folding knife connected hard with the sentry's throat, and as the man started to crumple downward, Mahovsky already had him by the neck and shoulders, dragging the body into the trees.

Frost grinned at his old friend. Mahovsky, in a hoarse stage whisper, smiling, was saying, "See—nothin' to it, huh?''

Frost shook his head.

The simplest way to reach the grounds undetected, to penetrate toward the parked eighteen wheelers carrying the guidance equipment, was to take out as many of the perimeter guards as possible. And methodically now, they began.

Frost came up on the second man, some twenty-yards distant from the first, but this one facing the trees, not the encampment.

Frost, the double edged boot knife in his teeth, the KG-9 slung across his back, inhaled, focusing his concentration on the tree behind the man who was his target. Slowly, Frost walked in a crouch toward the man from the side, stepping cautiously to avoid the sound of a tree branch breaking, or the rustling of leaves. Such work was better done at night, Frost realized—but there was no time to wait for night. Frost stared at the tree, only seeing the man he wanted to kill in his peripheral vision.

He was less than a half-dozen yards from the man now.

Slowly, he raised his right fist, snatching the knife by the catspaw surfaced handle, his fist balling around it for the right grip. Slowly, he raised his left hand, outstretching his left arm, the fingers of the hand slightly curled.

He started to run.

The sentry started to turn, Frost jumping toward the man, then twisting his body, throwing his weight back as he stabbed the spear pointed blade down into the sentry's throat.

He could feel the blade dodge against a bone, then penetrate deeper, Frost's left hand over the mouth, stifling the scream, feeling the man's spit on his palm as he pulled the sentry back, twisting out the knife, then slicing it across the throat, ear to ear. He let the head drop and gave the body a final tug to get it out of sight.

Mahovsky was ahead of him, already working on the next man.

As Frost passed, at a distance, further back in the trees, he could see his friend's hands move, a rolling motion, perhaps the wind the hands made making the sentry hear him or feel him and start to wheel around. The right fist flashed out into the sentry's face, the left following it, knotting around the throat, crushing the adam's apple.

Frost moved on, to the fourth man.

The man was looking away from him. Frost shrugged and broke into a low run, reaching out for the back of the man's head as the man started to turn. Frost's left fist knotted in the man's hair, snapping the head back as his right fist hammered the knife into the right kidney, his left hand sliding down across the face to cover the mouth and stifle the scream. Frost withdrew the knife, raking it across the sentry's throat.

He pulled the man back into the trees and started for his next target.

Mahovsky was already at work. Frost could see the body falling, having heard nothing. Frost picked his target, starting up on the man.

Frost froze, the man sneezing, looking into the trees as he did.

Their eyes met.

Frost swung the KG-9 assault pistol into position, his left hand sliding the bolt knob out of the safety notch, letting it fly forward to bolt open position. His right fist knotted around the pistol grip, shoving the gun forward against the pressure of the sling, the first finger of his right hand squeezing the trigger once, then once again, the sounds ear splitting in the silence of the woods. The sentry, his M-16 into position, fell backward suddenly.

Out of the corner of his eye, Frost could see Mahovsky. One of the sentrymen, on Frost's far left, was starting to swing toward Frost, his assault rifle coming up. But Mahovsky's right hand was flashing from under the short leather jacket he wore, the dully gleaming customized Smith revolver in his right fist, the heavy thudding sound of the gun going off, then firing again. Frost's KG-9 was swinging on line for the sentry as well, the pops of his 9mm drowned out in the booming sound of the .45.

"Six down," Frost snarled, starting into a dead run toward the edge of the tree line, "and only ninety four or so to go!"

Mahovsky was running, his KG-9 in his right fist, the customized revolver in his left. Frost glancing back at his friend once, then dropping to his knees, firing the KG-9, his left fist locked on the ventilated barrel shroud, his right fist pumping the trigger as three men charged toward him.

One, two, three—Frost pushed himself up to his feet and kept running, hearing the booming sound of Mahovsky's revolver twice more, then a long, semi-automatic burst from the KG-9, as Frost jumped over the body of the nearest of the three men he'd just shot.

Men—some women as well—were running toward him now from the three semi-trailers, but a cordon of men had formed around the center of the three as Frost faced them—either Chapmann and Dean were amazingly clever or that was the trailer with the guidance override equipment.

"That one, Ron!" Frost shouted to Mahovsky, wheeling, cutting down two more men as he turned. Mahovsky was surrounded by five men and Frost couldn't shoot for fear of hitting his friend.

As the five men started to close, Mahovsky simultaneously loosed a burst from the KG-9, firing the customized Smith & Wesson with his left hand, his right foot kicking up and out, catching one of the men in the face.

Four of the men down now, Frost could shoot, his KG-9 burping twice, the last man going down. "Look out Hank!"

It was Mahaovsky shouting and Frost hit the dirt, going into a roll, the ground where he'd stood erupting as a grenade impacted. On his back, the KG-9 held in both his fists, he fired the pistol out, pumping the trigger until the bolt closed on an empty chamber. Frost snatched at one of the three spare magazines in his trouser band, dumping the empty onto the dirt and ramming the fresh one home. He snapped open the bolt, then started firing, two men coming at him in a rush. Frost rolled, the ground beside him chewing up under the impact of a burst of assault rifle fire. Frost, on his back again, fired between his spread apart feet, two rounds popping into the forehead of the nearest man, the second man crumbling.

Frost assumed Mahovsky had gotten him.

The one-eyed man was on his feet now, snatching the Browning High Power from the holster under his left arm, awkwardly with his left hand, but jacking back the hammer. He started to run again, hearing a voice behind him, "Frost!"

Frost wheeled—Mahovsky was shouting something Frost couldn't hear. But Frost could see his friend's right hand, pulling back like a major league pitcher, a dark object sailing from it. Frost followed it with his eye.

The nearest of the three trucks exploded, the doors popping open.

Mahovsky was underhanding one of the grenades now and Frost, stuffing the KG-19 under his left arm for an instant, caught it, pulling the pin with his teeth. "Ouch!" Frost hated pulling grenade pins with his teeth—despite the movie image only masochists and desperate men did it. He was desperate.

Frost lobbed the grenade toward a concentration of men spraying toward him with assault rifle fire.

He felt something tearing at his leg as he hurled the grenade, rolling into the dirt.

The grenade detonated, Frost looking up, bodies spilled around the ground.

"I got more—this sucker was loaded with

'em," Mahovsky shouted, lobbing another grenade skyward, the grenade impacting into another group of riflemen.

Mahovsky was underhanding more of the grenades. Frost rolled onto his back, catching one, then another. There was blood oozing out of a hole in his pants legs but he couldn't really feel the wound.

Frost rolled onto his stomach, pushing himself up on his left hand, the pin on the first grenade out, his right arm drawn back, then the grenade leaving his hand, toward the rear of the truck hit with the earlier grenade.

It was a lucky shot and Frost knew it, the grenade hitting inside the truck.

There was an instant that seemed like eternity, men streaming from the truck, then the grenade exploding, a fireball whooshing out of the rear of the truck, peeling away the metal.

Mahovsky had an assault rifle in each hand now, firing them in alternating three-shot bursts at the men and women exiting the truck trailer.

Frost pushed himself to his feet—now the leg wound hurt—and he started to run.

The center trailer was still intact, men clambering toward the roof of it, assault rifles slung on their backs.

Frost pulled the pin on the second grenade he had, hauling back his arm to toss it.

"Grenade!" someone shouted, the men scrambling down from the roof of the truck trailer, but Frost didn't throw the grenade, holding it instead, running, dodging bursts of automatic weapons fire, throwing himself down behind the still burning nearer trailer, lobbing the grenade underhand toward the center trailer.

It exploded as it touched the ground, about ten yards from the center trailer, bodies sailing skyward, only parts of bodies coming down.

Frost fired the KG-9 dry, knocking down more than a half-dozen of Dean's and Chapmann's men, rolling onto his back to swap sticks.

Frost heard something behind him, spun onto his stomach and stuffed the Browning out in his left fist, firing once, once more then once again, cutting down a man firing an assault rifle, coming at him in a dead run.

Mahovsky was still on his feet, firing the twin assault rifles, advancing slowly toward the center of the camp.

The gun in Mahovsky's right hand went dry, then the one in his left, cutting down six men, a seventh still on his feet.

The man threw his assault rifle away, coming at Mahovsky in a rush with a bayonet.

Mahovsky seemed to swell his chest again, taking in air, dropping both empty rifles, stepping back, his right hand turning in a small arc, the big lockblade folding knife appearing there.

The man with the bayonet slowed his charge.

Frost popped two rounds out of the Browning, cutting down a man trying to cross from the center trailer to the far trailer. His KG-9 was loaded again.

Frost looked back at Mahovsky. The man with the bayonet feigned a move, a lunge, Mahovsky stomping a half step back, turning, the knife flashing out as if it were on some sort of pivot, the blade slicing, catching the setting sun, blood spurting from the man's cheek.

The man stepped back, reaching for his pistol, Mahovsky sidestepping, making a sweeping kick to the man's face. The man went down.

Frost heard a burst of assault rifle fire, turned and started pumping the KG-9—six men were rushing him. His first bursts nailed two, two more took cover by the center trailer, two more were still coming. The KG-9 in Frost's right fist, the Browning High Power in his left, Frost fired both guns simultaneously, the man on his right spinning, falling, the man on his left looking as though someone had pulled a rug out from under him, his feet staying back, his body lurching forward, his body slapping almost horizontally into the ground.

Frost dumped the magazine for the High Power, ramming a fresh one home, then did the same for the KG-9, but stuffing the half-spent magazine into his belt.

The one-eyed man pushed to his feet.

There was assault rifle fire from his right. He glanced that way as he started to run. Mahovsky with two M-16s, firing them again, advancing.

Frost looked skyward—there were two helicopters, and he knew why they were coming.

And one of the choppers had a submachinegunner leaning out of the bubble dome, firing.

Frost was near the center truck now, diving toward the ground as the ground beside him ate up under the automatic weapons fire.

Frost started firing the KG-9, the Browning shoved into his belt, the ventilated barrel shroud of the semi-automatic 9mm in his left fist, the pistol grip in his right. Two rounds, two more, then three, then two. He could see the helicopter's dome spiderwebbing under the impact of the 115-grain JHPs, but the subgunner still fired.

Frost pumped the KG-9's trigger again and again, the roaring of the helicopter rotors overhead maddening in its intensity. The subgunner was hitting into the ground beside Frost's body now as Frost pumped one more long, semi-automatic burst. The little assault pistol bucking in his hands, the subgunner seeming to stall in freeze frame, then topple head first from the helicopter. The machine was backing off as Frost fired.

He swapped to his last full magazine, glancing at the black luminous face of the Rolex Sea-Dweller on his left wrist. It was five forty—if the guidance of the space shuttle hadn't already been overridden, it would be in seconds. And the computers for the guidance system were yards away.

The one-eyed man rammed the magazine in place, the leg wound hurting a little now. Mahovsky was still walking and firing, a hail of bullets around him. Frost pushed to his feet, running toward the center semi-trailer truck, firing the KG-9. There were too many men and too few minutes to go.

Chapter 37

Frost froze, despite the gunfire directed at him. He could see Eva Chapmann, running from the center semi-trailer, her blonde hair blowing out straight behind her, wearing combat boots and fatigues, a submachinegun in her hands, firing despite her left arm held in a sling. And there was gunfire going toward her. She hit the dirt, rolled and fired a burst from the subgun toward the trailer.

Frost fired the KG-9 at her, missing. She was running toward the second helicopter, landed now on the far side of the shallow valley, beyond the radio dish.

Frost started to change direction, to chase after her, but stopped. He hadn't seen Creighton Dean—Dean would be punching the buttons now, flipping the switches, whatever the hell someone did when they operated a computer, Frost thought. And in twenty minutes give or take, maybe a couple hundred thousand, maybe as many as a million people would be dead or injured.

Frost spat toward Eva Chapmann, twisting on his feet, turning toward the trailer, going into a dead run.

There were men shooting at him and Frost was shooting back, running. He fell once, not knowing, not feeling if he'd been hit again, then pushed himself to his feet, still running. He caught sight of Mahovsky, moving in, just one assault rifle now, cutting his way through. Suddenly, Mahovsky stopped shooting, doubling over and falling to the ground.

Two men were coming at Mahovsky, Frost stalling in his run, hitting the dirt to shoot.

But Mahovsky had the revolver he'd hand made in his right fist and was firing it.

One shot—one man went down. A second shot, a second man.

Then Mahovsky's right arm stretched back and something dark sailed into the air.

Frost picked himself up, running, diving to the dirt as the grenade exploded.

Dirt, gravel—blood and flesh—it streamed down on him as he pushed himself up, the path to the center trailer almost clear now.

"Go—go, man!"

Frost could hear his old friend shouting—and he did it—go.

Two men on his right, a burst from the KG-9, then another burst. Two men dead ahead. Frost fired the KG-9 again, then again, and they were—dead ahead.

Another grenade went off, too close, his ears ringing, but more of Chapmann's and Dean's men going down.

The end of the trailer, the doors open, was less than a dozen yards away.

In the center of the open doors was Phillip Piersen—the bodyguard, the killer, the kidnaper. A submachine gun—absently Frost thought it was an Uzi—was in Pierson's hands, firing.

Frost hit the dirt, feeling something ripping at his left arm, rolling as the ground chewed up where he'd been, firing the KG-9 across the top of his body, upside down. The hot brass pelted his face as he pumped the trigger. He rolled again, the KG-9 still going, Piersen still firing, then seeming to twitch.

The submachinegun in Piersen's hands went wild as Piersen spun, twisted, started to fall, the subgun still firing as Piersen slammed down to the ground.

Frost was on his feet, the KG-9 empty. Frost snatched the Browning High Power out, the Pachmayr gripped pistol in his right fist like a lifeline as he ran the last dozen yards.

The one-eyed man jumped, throwing himself forward, sliding into the rear of the trailer, across the wooden floor.

Creighton Dean, a Walther P-38 pistol in his right hand, was wheeling away from a console. In the background, there was a digital diode printout on a black screen, the numerals red like blood.

The numbers "2:43," appeared there. Frost didn't think it was the time.

Frost fired and Dean fired, Dean spinning around on his feet, lurching back against the consoles, looking to Frost like he was reaching with his left hand for a large black switch, like an electrical power switch.

Frost fired the Browning, once, twice, three times, into Dean's face and neck, the would be mass murderer, the financer of Marcus and Eva Chapmann slumping, then sliding across the panel, dropping to the floor, rolling once and then still. Frost pulled himself up.

The diode counter read 1:59." It changed as Frost watched it. "1:58."

"Jesus," Frost rasped. "That's the time until—"

He didn't finish the words, running toward the consoles, staring at the buttons. The tapes were reeling off and up, the lights and buttons and switches flickering. He started to touch one, drawing his hand back. "1:34."

"Dammit!"

The one-eyed man was shouting to himself.

He went to touch a toggle switch. Had to be the time until the takeover of the guidance system, Frost told himself, then once the new program overrode the NASA program, diverting the shuttle would be irretrievable.

"0:58"

Frost felt like a caveman in a laundromat—which button to press?

"0:51. . . . 0:50. . . . 0:49"

He saw a red button—red buttons were always important.

"0:42"

He pushed the red button and nothing happened that he could see, the diodes still counting.

"0:37"

"Thirty seven seconds!"

He looked at the diode counter: "0:29"

Frost rammed the half-empty Browning High Power toward the tapes, unreeling, reeling. He leveled the pistol at the output reel.

"0:18"

The one-eyed man fired, pumping the Metalifed High Power's trigger until the slide locked open, the plexiglas over the tape reels shattering, the reels themselves breaking apart, the tape spilling out across the console. The lights on the console went out, the switches that were illuminated died and the tape reels stopped turning, all power for the machine seeming to suddenly have died.

The diode counter was still working. "0:04".

Frost reached down and flipped the big black switch that looked like it belonged on an electric chair.

The diodes flickered out, the screen blank. "Zero zero four," Frost smiled. "Three higher and I would've been a big hit. Can't win 'em all."

Frost wheeled, the empty Browning in his hand. It was Mahovsky, grinning, his left hand dripping blood as he stood in the trailer doors.

"The blonde lady got away. But I whacked that helicopter you started chewing on. Gotta do this again sometime, Frost."

"Uh-huh," the one-eyed man nodded. "Uh-huh."

Chapter 38

"Well, well, well—the one-eyed man rides again, huh?"

Frost grinned down at the man in the hospital bed. "O'Hara—too bad they didn't shoot out your vocal cords."

"Yeah—don't ya just wish," the steely-eyed FBI man snapped.

Frost studied his face—thinner than the last time Frost had seen him, the jawline more pronounced, the eyes a little deeper set.

"What's ya lookin' at?"

"I was just wondering how somebody looked after a coma. You doin' okay?"

"Yeah—the doctor says I'll be outa here in no time—"

"Bullshit. The doctor said you'll be in here for another three weeks while those gunshot wounds heal up and they make certain there won't be any residual effects from the concussion."

"You're spyin' on me, Frost—always gotta

know what I'm doin'. I guess I'm a model to ya—you look up to me. Noble guardian of our nation's security, Federal lawman, the whole bit.''

"Nuts," Frost laughed.

"I hear you lost the biggee though—wouldn't a done that if I'd been there. Lost little old Eva.''

"I'll find her—we killed Creighton Dean, that creep Pierson who worked for him, a ton of their people. We stopped the guidance equipment before it could divert the space shuttle and hit downtown Manhattan.''

"I coulda done that.''

Frost nodded, smiling. "I know you coulda—but, had to keep myself busy.''

"You goin' after that broad Eva Chapmann—what's that nickname she's got?''

"The Deathwitch—yeah. If I don't, she'll come after me, maybe go after Bess to get to me. Might even come after you. She's like that.''

"Well—good luck to ya. You wouldn't wanna wait three weeks or so, huh? I got a little vacation left. Probably give me some time off to recuperate anyway. What about it?''

"I can't wait. Eva Chapmann's probably got somethin' cookin'—only figures. The longer I leave goin' after her, the colder the trail'll get. Gotta go. Fact, I got tickets to London for a plane leaving in two hours. Just stopped off to see how you were doing.''

"Surprised that battle-axe nurse let you in.''

"I got your friend Kelsoe to call up and fix it.''

"Yeah—Kelsoe's okay. You gonna see Bess when you hit on London?''

"Yeah—take me a day or so to get a line on tracking Eva. I can spend it with Bess."

"Well—say hello to her, huh? Tell her old O'Hara of the FBI sends his best."

"I will," Frost nodded.

"Shoot it to me straight, Frost—you think you'll get Eva Chapmann? Looks like she stashes gunmen under every rock."

"She's got a few," Frost agreed.

"You think you'll get her?"

"I think I'll get her. What do you think?"

"Well—when I heard about all this with space shuttle and a kidnapped PhD and automobile chases, all this crap. Well, I said to myself, there are some guys who draw trouble like rotten meat draws flies."

"Thanks," Frost murmured.

"No—I don't mean it like an insult."

"How do you mean it?"

"I mean—well, I figure you'll get this Chapmann broad—one of these days anyway. But after that, I can't see you sittin' at some typewriter someplace and writin' your memoirs, you know what I mean? Naw—you'll keep doin' this rough-tough stuff. Somebody gets a mercenary contract you like, or that stiff Andy Deacon needs you for some executive protection job. You agree?"

"Ya know—the one thing I really detest about you, Mike?"

"What?"

"You're usually right." Frost shook hands with his friend and walked out.

Chapter 39

Hank Frost kissed the nipples on Bess's breasts—first the left one, closer to him, then leaned across her body and kissed the right one. She opened her eyes.

"Frost . . ."

"We've got one more day before I go—figured let's get up early and use it."

"We don't have to get up though," she whispered, wrapping her arms around his neck.

Frost, his left hand knotted in the blonde hair at the nape of her neck, his right hand on her left breast, kissed her slightly parted lips, felt her tongue searching against his. He moved his tongue against hers—then she did what she frequently did—she bit it.

"Ouch!"

"Just wanted to make sure you were awake," she smiled.

"There are better ways to tell," Frost rasped, sliding between her thighs, feeling her hands against him. He slipped inside her, arching her back up under him, hearing her whisper, "What?"

He looked into her face—her eyes were closed and her lips were drawn in a thin, happy smile. "I was saying the name of the thing I like best—Frost . . ."

They showered together and dressed, Bess remembering there was a little restaurant not far from her apartment that'd she'd always wanted Frost to try—a sort of combination of American and English food served on Sundays—it was Sunday morning—smorgasbord style.

Frost acquiesced, but preferring her cooking better—it had something to do with who prepared it, he thought.

They took the stairs down to the ground floor and started to walk, the street all but deserted.

"Frost—maybe she learned her lesson—and before you tell me, I know. Women always say things like that."

"They do," the one-eyed man smiled.

"Well—I just wish you—"

"I know that," Frost told her. "Maybe if you weren't wishing that I wouldn't feel I had to go."

She stopped walking, looking at him, huddling her shoulders in the trenchcoat she wore. "What do you mean?"

"Just a matter of time, kid—before she comes after me or after you. Wouldn't be any kind of a life. You know that."

"I know," she whispered, then leaned up on

her toes, her high heels off the ground and kissed him.

"Come on—let's go eat. Where is that place?"

"Just around—"

Frost shoved her away, hearing the screeching sound of the tires as the black Jaguar sedan rolled around the corner, coming too close to the curb and on the wrong side of the street. He looked at the car, the rear window rolling down, then grabbed Bess by the shoulders, dragging her, running her toward the storefront.

He could already hear it, the submachinegun starting to spit, the pavement starting to crackle as the bullets impacted. The glass in the storefront was shattering and Frost pushed Bess down, cursing the fact he didn't have a gun.

"Stay down!" Frost shouted.

The car was even with them now and glass from the storefront windows on both sides was shattering all around them. Frost covered Bess with his body, tucking down as the subgunner in the rear window of the Jaguar fired one more burst.

"No-o-o!" Frost felt the slugs impact, a hot, tearing feeling in his right shoulder and forearm, in his right ribcage and his upper right thigh.

He was moving with the impact of the slugs, powerless to stop himself, falling, jerking, twisting. He threw his left hand in front of his face as he lurched head first through the shattered window on his right, glass falling, raining around him.

The one-eyed man moved his left hand—he

could feel it bleeding, cut from the glass, hear the glass tinkling down as he tried to move his legs, his left arm.

"Frost!"

Frost opened his eye. Bess was standing there, trying to climb into the store window after him. There wasn't any blood on her, but her face was white, whiter than he'd ever seen it. "Frost!"

"Stay out—you'll get cut!"

"The hell, the hell with that," she stammered, kneeling down beside him in the glass.

"You'll run your stockings—"

"Shut up—" and she bent over him, kissing his mouth.

He could hear sirens in the distance—police or an ambulance—maybe both, he hoped.

"I'm okay—you sound like I did, that time in Canada—"

"Frost . . ."

"The glass—"

"I don't care," and she took his head in her arms and rocked it against her abdomen.

She was crying.

For that—that Bess cried—if for nothing else, Frost was going to kill Eva Chapmann. And the harder the Deathwitch died the better.